The

Quilting Bee

a romance by the sea

De-ann Black

Abby leaves her life in the city behind and moves to a lovely cottage by the sea in a beautiful village in Scotland. She plans to bake cakes and sew quilts.

Romance isn't on her agenda, especially as she's been unlucky in love in the past. But when she joins the ladies quilting bee, they encourage her to believe that romance is brewing when a couple of the local men take an interest in her.

While setting up her quilting and baking business in the cottage, Abby becomes a busy bee, but will she make time to take a chance on love?

Published 2019

The Quilting Bee: a romance by the sea

ISBN: 9781078075794

Also by De-ann Black (Romance, Action/Thrillers & Children's books). See her Amazon Author page or website for further details about her books, screenplays, illustrations, art and fabric designs.

www.De-annBlack.com

Romance:

Embroidery Cottage
The Dressmaker's Cottage
The Sewing Shop
Heather Park
The Tea Shop by the Sea
The Bookshop by the Seaside
The Sewing Bee
The Quilting Bee
Snow Bells Wedding
Snow Bells Christmas
Summer Sewing Bee
The Chocolatier's Cottage
Christmas Cake Chateau
The Beemaster's Cottage
The Sewing Bee By The Sea
The Flower Hunter's Cottage

The Christmas Knitting Bee
The Sewing Bee & Afternoon Tea
The Vintage Sewing & Knitting Bee
Shed In The City
The Bakery By The Seaside
Champagne Chic Lemonade Money
The Christmas Chocolatier
The Christmas Tea Shop & Bakery
The Vintage Tea Dress Shop In Summer
Oops! I'm The Paparazzi
The Bitch-Proof Suit

Action/Thrillers:

Agency Agenda
Love Him Forever.
Someone Worse.

Electric Shadows.
The Strife Of Riley.
Shadows Of Murder.

Colouring books:

Summer Garden. Spring Garden. Autumn Garden. Sea Dream. Festive Christmas. Christmas Garden. Flower Bee. Wild Garden. Faerie Garden Spring. Flower Hunter. Stargazer Space. Bee Garden.

Embroidery books:

Floral Garden Embroidery Patterns
Floral Spring Embroidery Patterns
Christmas & Winter Embroidery Patterns
Floral Nature Embroidery Designs
Scottish Garden Embroidery Designs

Contents

CHAPTER ONE

Abby drove along the narrow country road that led to her new life by the sea. She could see the water sparkling through the trees as she wound her way to the coast. The Scottish countryside spilled down to the edge of the bay in a patchwork of green fields neatly bordered by hedgerows. Houses and cottages were scattered across the landscape, mainly hidden from view within niches of trees and greenery, until the expanse of sea opened up to reveal a quaint little village sitting happily along the coastline.

Boats bobbed in the tiny harbour and a row of shops painted in pastel tones of pink, peppermint and vanilla reminded her of ice cream on a summer's day. The sun glinted off the water and she shielded her eyes to follow the directions to the cottage. And there it was...a beautiful cottage overlooking the sea.

She parked her car as near to the cottage as the road would allow, and stepped out to breathe in the sea air. The breeze blew through her shoulder–length, silky brown hair and she felt the warmth of the sun on her pale features. The excitement she felt outweighed her trepidation. Moving from the city had been impulsive, but the urge to take a chance on a fresh start encouraged her to leave her past behind. This included her job at the advertising agency where she'd been overworked and overlooked yet again for promotion. The company praised her work, and she earned substantial bonuses, but she was stuck in a rut and it didn't seem as if she was going to make her way up the corporate ladder any time soon. Her bosses hinted it was due to her lack of networking, of not attending all the parties and functions necessary for her to become promotion material. She admitted she wasn't a social butterfly, but she'd attended most of the parties she was expected to be at and hadn't complained once.

Not being a party girl didn't stop her enjoying herself, but her idea of a great night was to snuggle up on the sofa, after having a home cooked dinner, sew quilts and watch her favourite TV shows or films. Dating someone tall, handsome and loyal, with an emphasis on the loyal, was of course on her wish list. When it came to love and romance she'd never found the right man, and had a tendency to attract the wrong type on a few occasions. Often it was easier not to date two–timing, traitorous weasels and concentrate on her career

1

and sew quilts. It wasn't the ideal plan, and as the months and years flicked past, she realised she was stuck in a rut and needed to force herself to find the type of life she longed for. Owning her own quilt shop was up there on her wish list, along with moving away from the city to enjoy a rural lifestyle.

When the letter arrived from her great aunt's solicitor informing her she'd inherited a cottage by the sea in the Scottish Highlands her first reaction was to tell them she couldn't accept their offer. The cottage sounded lovely, and so did her great aunt Netta even though they'd never actually met, but being the only relative left that might be capable of taking on the responsibility of the cottage, the offer had been given to her. But it came with conditions. One in particular. The cottage was a small bakery business, supplying the local tea shop and grocery store with cakes, and she must promise to continue this for at least one year, baking and selling cakes. If she couldn't make it work, then she was free to do what she wanted with the cottage including selling it.

Baking cakes was a far cry from working in advertising, but it was nearer to living a crafty life sewing quilts. She could cook and enjoyed baking. Whipping up a Victoria sponge filled with raspberry jam and buttercream was easy enough. However, baking to a standard suitable for selling to customers was a whole different league. What if people didn't like her penchant for adding coffee and a pinch of chili to her chocolate cakes? Would her preference for sticky toffee cupcakes drizzled with caramel meet with their approval? She loved making carrot cake, but would they frown on her topping it with slices of crystallised lemon? Her cake baking repertoire was small but reliable, rather like she was. After much consideration, she supposed she could give it a go...

It was a wrench to pry herself out of that rut and adhere to the terms of the agreement. Before plucking up the nerve to throw in the towel at the ad agency, she'd been working on an advertising campaign that drained every ounce of energy from her. When it was done and the clients were enthusiastic about the outcome, her immediate boss helped her decide what to do next. Not that he knew she was thinking of running off to the Highlands. She hadn't told anyone. So when he'd tapped her on the shoulder with the praiseworthy report and grudgingly grinned that she'd done well, that was it. She grabbed that towel and threw it into the ring with determination and gusto, picked up her things and left the building. The traffic in Glasgow had sounded angry that day when she stepped out of the agency and stood there in the light drizzle pondering her future. It was as if it sensed she was about to leave the city in the lurch and drive off further north than she'd been in years.

And now here she was. She'd better make a go of it, she warned herself, because the welcome mat wasn't waiting for her back home in the city.

She stepped through the long grass into the cottage garden. She'd been given a virtual tour of the cottage, and apart from figuring out how to use a log burning stove, she reckoned she could handle staying there. Making a living, money, well...that was something she would have to master. In the month it had taken to organise moving to the coast, from signing the agreement to leaving her rented flat, she'd taken a short and intensive course in baking to hone her skills. She'd learned to make fluffier scones with buttermilk, and a variety of cakes from lemon drizzle cake to chocolate fudge cake and shortbread to Scottish tea bread.

She took a moment to breathe and look around her. She'd done what she'd set out to do, at least partially. Now the challenge was to make it work, and she was determined to give it all she had.

While she was gazing at the cottage, the feeling that someone was watching her shot through her back, and she glanced round to see the tall, fit figure of a man with dark hair wearing charcoal grey training gear run along the far end of the bay and disappear into the trees. Blink and he'd gone, as if he'd never been there. A handsome shadow of a man.

She'd sensed someone looking at her, and wondered if it had been him. As a newcomer she expected to attract looks of suspicion, but hoped she'd be welcomed. A few other people were further along near the shops, but she didn't think they'd even noticed her arrive, though there was a man with a shock of burnished gold hair in one of the fields, striding across it like he owned it — a strapping figure in cords, a jacket and waistcoat all in neutral colours of moss green, dun, ochre and sand. He looked like old money although he was only in his thirties. His clothes were casual, work–worn perhaps, those of a gentleman who participated in the daily labour of the land rather than left the hard graft to others. Had he seen her? Maybe...

She shrugged off the thought of this and looked again at the cottage with its whitewashed exterior. The two front windows shone in the sunlight and offered a view of the sea. The garden was quite substantial and surrounded the property on all sides. She liked that it provided privacy and people couldn't just walk right past her cottage and peer in at her.

A local housekeeper had been tending to the cleaning and maintenance of the property. A new mattress for the bed and fresh linen had been ordered. Packing up her belongings in her flat had been easy as she'd rented it furnished and hadn't accumulated anything of value except a few personal items and her quilting. She loved her sewing machine and it was carefully tucked in the boot of her car, cushioned with quilts.

Taking a deep breath, she started to unpack the car and carry her things inside. A set of keys had been posted to her and she unlocked the front door and stepped into the loveliest cottage she could've hoped for.

The lounge was homely. A couch was set against one wall and two armchairs were on either side of the fireplace. The furniture was old but well cared for and she loved the vintage style of everything. Overall, the cottage was bright and airy. The lounge walls were a light cream, and patio doors let the sunlight in and led on to the back garden.

She put the things she was carrying down on a table and pushed the patio doors open wide, feeling the warmth of the day and the scent of the flowers in the garden flood in. The lawn stretched all the way to the fence that separated her garden from the field where she'd seen the man striding across it. Flowers and border plants created a colourful array around the lawn. Brambles grew near part of the hedging, and rambling roses had taken it upon themselves to clamber over the shed. An apple tree stood in the far corner, as if on guard, and created a niche where she could sit sheltered from the elements. Two garden chairs and a table sat underneath the branches, and she imagined this was a favourite spot where her great aunt relaxed after a busy day baking. Perhaps she'd do the same.

She went back inside and wandered through to the bedroom where a new mattress was on the bed along with a pile of folded new linen, as promised.

The cottage was fresh and clean and the sea air blew inside as she left the front door open, popping in and out to transport all her belongings.

The kitchen was amazing, and a bit intimidating because it was clearly designed to cope with a busy baking business and extended out into the garden.

Recipe books lined a shelf, and flicking through them she saw they contained her great aunt Netta's special recipes, hand written and tucked into the pages, along with traditional recipes. Another promise agreed on — Abby would include in her baking list several of the special recipes that were favourites with the local customers. These included the classic Victoria sponge cakes and traditional fruitcake.

She put the books back up on the shelf and tried not to panic. She could do this, she could, definitely, probably.

Once she was settled in she figured out how to work the wood burning stove. At her bakery course she'd learned how to properly clean a cooker and other handy methods for running an efficient kitchen.

She checked the cupboards for food supplies, but they were empty. Instructions on what items were needed for baking had been given to her, and according to the notes she could order these from the local grocery shop. She scribbled her own grocery list of things she needed, but before going shopping she flopped down on the sofa and finished the flask of tea she'd brought with her.

Euan breezed into Minnie's grocery shop and looked at Bracken snuggled up in his basket behind the counter. Being so tall, he could see right over it, and the dog was lying on a quilt that Minnie had made for him.

'What can I get for you, Euan?' said Minnie, a cheerful looking woman in her fifties with her brown hair pinned up in bun. Her shop stocked a wide range of grocery products and was as neat and tidy as Minnie.

'I was wondering if Bracken would like to go for a walk along the shore with me?' He hoped by emphasising the dog's name this would gain his attention, but the dog seemed quite relaxed on his quilt in the basket. He was a mix of breeds including spaniel, a mid–

sized dog with black, white and brown colouring and floppy ears. He had a good nature and enjoyed customers paying him attention.

She glanced at her dog. 'He's all cosy in his basket. He's been chasing bumblebees in one of the fields this morning and he's tuckered out.'

'I'm sure he's still got some bounce left in him, haven't you, Bracken?'

Minnie eyed Euan cautiously. 'Are you okay?'

'Yes, I just—'

She put her hand up to stop him from continuing. 'Don't lie. You're up to something. What is it?'

He sighed heavily. Minnie knew him only too well. 'I need to borrow Bracken so I can walk past the old bakery cottage without looking like I'm spying on the young woman who appears to have moved in.'

Minnie's expression brightened. 'Oh, so she's arrived.'

'Yes, so if I could just take Bracken for a quick jaunt along the shore.'

Snoring from the basket made him pause.

Minnie laughed.

Euan sighed. 'I thought Bracken would want to go for walkies.'

The dog's ears twitched, and he perked up.

'Did you see that? He's keen to go, aren't you, boy?'

Minnie was about to shake her head, but the dog stretched and hoisted himself up and looked at Euan.

Minnie handed Euan the lead. 'Good luck getting him to walk all the way there and back. He's knackered.'

Euan clipped the lead on to the dog's collar. 'Do you know anything about the woman?' he asked Minnie.

'I heard she's accepted the cottage, but I don't know many details about her. Apparently she's from the city and worked in advertising. Josh's housekeeper, Pearl, has been tending to the cottage as his firm is handling the legalities, but she's been told not to pass on any gossip about the young woman, especially to me.'

Euan nodded, taking in this information. Minnie was known as a bit of a gossipmonger, but a well intentioned meddler.

'I won't be long,' he assured her, and led Bracken outside.

The dog became more energetic as the fresh air hit his nostrils. The fur on his floppy ears wafted in the breeze as they hurried along the shore towards Abby's cottage.

Euan couldn't see her, but the cottage door was open. He muttered to himself, wondering how to gain her attention without looking nosy.

As he hesitated, a sea bird flew past and landed in Abby's front garden. Bracken chased after it, and although he'd never caught anything other than the odd fly, his enthusiasm and energy tugged the lead from Euan's grasp.

He ran after the dog as it bounded into Abby's garden.

Abby tucked her grocery list into her jacket pocket. She'd changed into a pair of grey jeans and a white top and was on her way out the front door when a bundle of energetic fur came scurrying towards her.

'Well, hello there.' She smiled at the dog, unfazed by the situation. It was only when Euan spoke that she noticed him. She was too busy lavishing attention on the dog.

'Sorry, he got away from me,' Euan apologised while his senses were struck by the lovely young woman standing in front of him. From a distance she'd looked pleasant, but he'd clearly underestimated how pretty she was. More than anything, he hadn't expected to be affected by her, not like this. He didn't want to be attracted to her when he hoped to wangle the cottage from her. Guilt wrenched at his guts and he hated feeling like a low–life sneak.

She smiled at him, bright and open. 'What's your dog's name?'

He couldn't lie to her. So he told her the truth, or at least some of it. 'His name is Bracken, but he's not my dog. He belongs to the owner of the grocery shop. I'm Euan. I offered to take him for a run along the shore.'

'Oh, that was nice of you.' By now she was crouched down, ruffling the dog's fur and Bracken was nuzzling into her.

'I...eh...' He hated lying to her. Hated it like poison. 'I see you've moved in.'

Her lovely blue eyes looked up at him. 'Yes, the cottage belonged to my great aunt Netta. I inherited it.'

No lies from her. He bit his lip before he let one slip, or a half truth.

'I saw you walking across the field up there.' She pointed to where she'd seen him earlier.

'That's my field. It backs on to your cottage garden. I...' he hesitated, wondering whether to come right out and tell her he wanted her cottage and was willing to pay more than it was worth.

She spoke to him while still smiling at the dog. 'Yes?'

He reached for the lead and gently pulled Bracken back to heel. 'I'm sorry. I shouldn't have intruded.' And he hurried off before she could say anything.

She watched him stride away with the dog. He was a handsome one, no doubt about that, but there was a look in those hazel eyes of his that made her wonder if he was up to something...

Halfway home, Bracken seemed to run out of steam and flopped down on the grass. No amount of cajoling or gentle tugging could get him to put a spurt on, or even a meander. Needing to get the dog back to the shop, Euan picked up the pooch and carried him.

Minnie laughed when he walked in with Bracken in his arms and put him down carefully in his basket. He unclipped the lead and handed it to her.

'I'm glad you're amused,' Euan told her.

Seeing that her dog was safe and sound, Minnie was eager to know what had happened. 'So, did you see her?'

'Yes, Bracken got her full attention, and she obviously loves dogs.'

'Did you find out any more information about her?'

'No, I didn't want to...' he broke off. 'I met her, and that was all.'

Minnie frowned at him. 'You didn't tell her you want the cottage?'

He looked down and scuffed his boots. 'No.'

'You've had your eye on that cottage for ages. Your grandfather helped build it. It's right on the edge of your field. You should've made her an offer for it.'

'I know, but she seemed so happy to have moved in. The timing wasn't right. I'll try again once she's settled in.'

Minnie gave him a knowing smile. 'Pretty is she?'

He tried to sound as if this hadn't crossed his mind. 'I suppose so.'

'What does she look like?'

He held up his hand to indicate that she barely came up to his shoulders. 'Quite small, slender, stylish in her own way, a city girl. She certainly doesn't look like she belongs here.'

At that moment the shop door opened and Abby walked in.

Euan grabbed a packet of biscuits and thrust them at Minnie. 'And I'll take a packet of custard creams.' He gave her a panicked look.

Minnie went along with the ruse and accepted the money for the biscuits.

Abby noticed Bracken was tucked up in his basket. 'Did he enjoy his walk?' she asked happily.

'He did,' said Euan, hoping she hadn't seen him lugging the dog back to the shop.

Minnie smiled at Abby. 'You must be our newcomer. I hear you've moved into Netta's cottage. I'm Minnie.'

'Yes, I'm Abby. I was hoping to place an order with you.' Abby showed her the list of items.

Minnie skimmed the list. 'I've got most of these in stock and could order the other items to be here in a day or two. We get regular deliveries.'

'That would be great,' said Abby.

'So, you're going to be busy baking then?' Minnie asked.

'I am. Do you have a list of cakes that Netta used to provide for you?'

Minnie opened a drawer under the counter. 'I've got it here.' She pulled out a piece of paper. 'The cakes and shortbread were always popular with customers.'

Abby snapped a copy of the items with her phone and handed the paper back to Minnie. 'I'll get these made for you. That's if you're still interested in them.'

'I'd definitely like to have the cakes and shortbread I used to buy. Are you a baker yourself?'

'It's part of the agreement. When I accepted the cottage I agreed to continue the baking business for at least a year.' Abby explained the details.

Euan was still lingering. 'Do you think you'll move back to the city, if you sell the cottage after a year?'

'I'm hoping to make a go of it here, especially with my quilting.'

Minnie's interest perked up. 'Oh, you're a quilter?'

'Yes, but I can bake.'

'I'm sure you can, Abby, but you'll have to come along and join in our quilting bee.'

'I'd love to.' The invitation appealed to her immediately. She'd occasionally been part of quilting evenings online, but never attended a quilting bee.

'We get together a couple of evenings a week at the tea shop,' Minnie explained. 'It's just along from here. There's a wee function room at the back of the tea shop and it's a sort of hub for local events. Gordon owns it, and he lets us keep a couple of our sewing machines there so we can set things up easily.'

'I'll certainly come along.'

'We've got a bee on tonight. It's short notice, but you'd be made welcome.'

'Okay, I'll pop along. What time?'

'Around seven and we finish about nine. Bring anything you're working on and meet the other members.'

'I'm working on a couple of quilts at the moment.'

As Abby and Minnie started to talk about quilting, this was Euan's cue to leave.

'I'll see you later.' He exited with his biscuits and an uneasy feeling that he'd been disingenuous.

'Cheer up, Euan,' Gordon said, walking towards him on his way to the grocery shop. Gordon matched Euan in height, but his build was leaner, broad shoulders tapering down to a toned torso and lean hips. Although he owned the tea shop and liked to partake in the cakes and pastries, he loved to swim, and there was barely a day went by when he didn't enjoy a dip in the sea regardless of the weather. This resulted in giving him a hardy physique and energy to work from early morning until often in the evenings. As a single man, he made his own hours, and luckily he lived and worked beside the sea that he loved so much.

Euan tried to lift the heavy frown from his brow and forced a smile. 'Fair warning — Minnie and Abby are talking about quilts, so if you're in a hurry to be served, it could take a while.'

Gordon grinned. 'Thanks for the heads–up.' He continued on, then said over his shoulder, 'Abby?'

Euan paused. 'She's moved into the bakery cottage. She's from the city. And she's coming along to the quilting bee tonight.'

'I'd better say hello then.' Gordon waved at Euan and went into the shop.

Minnie was talking about fabric. 'I order my fabric bundles online, and there's a great wee shop in the nearest town that sells a lovely selection of quilting cotton.' She stopped when she saw Gordon.

He smiled at her, but his attention was directed at Abby, though he tried to hide his immediate interest. 'Don't let me interrupt, Minnie. I'm just in for two jars of your homemade raspberry jam.' He picked them up from a shelf and flicked a glance at Abby.

Blue–green eyes that reminded her of the sea looked at her, and Abby felt herself smile. There was a warmth about this man. His tawny hair was lightened from the sun, and his handsome face lit up when he smiled back at her. Unexpectedly, her heart skipped a beat and she felt an attraction towards him. He wore a crisp white shirt, open at the neck, and classic dark trousers. He was clean–shaven, and there was nothing rough in either his manner or voice. He sounded pleasant and he was very good looking.

'This is Gordon,' Minnie said, delighted to introduce him. 'He owns the tea shop. Abby's our newcomer and she's coming along to the quilting bee tonight.'

Gordon stepped forward and extended his hand to Abby. 'Pleased to meet you. Euan says you've moved into Netta's bakery cottage.'

Abby shook hands with him, noting that his hands were elegant and he didn't crush her hand in his grip. She was about to tell him she'd inherited the cottage when Minnie jumped in with all the details.

'Abby's going to be baking cakes and all the other things we used to buy from Netta. She's taking over where her great aunt left off, so you'll be able to order the Victoria sponge cakes and shortbread from Abby now.'

Abby squirmed, feeling as if there was no way he could refuse. 'That's if you're interested,' Abby was quick to add.

Gordon was clearly interested. He handed the two jars of raspberry jam to Abby. 'In that case, these belong to you. I was going to bake the Victoria sponges for the bee tonight but if you're up for it, maybe you could do it. I'm going to be busy baking flans and scones.'

Abby stood there holding the two jars of jam and secretly panicking. 'I'd be happy to bake them,' she said, hoping she could figure out how to use the cooker in the cottage. Instructions had been left, and a cooker was a cooker, but she'd planned to have a trial run at using the ovens before actually baking cakes for customers.

'Two Victoria sponges would be ideal,' he said. 'I like to use Minnie's homemade jam. It's delicious.'

Abby clutched the jars. 'I'm sure it is.' She didn't doubt it. Even a glance at the jars showed they were packed with rich fruit, probably picked locally.

'I get the raspberries from Euan. He grows a wonderful selection of berry fruits and vegetables,' Minnie told her.

Gordon chimed–in. 'Euan's field backs on to your garden. That's why he's keen to buy the cottage from you.'

His words hung in the air for a second before they sunk in and hit Abby hard. As the realisation showed on her face, Gordon sensed he'd unintentionally let slip about Euan's motives. He tried to explain. 'He's wanted it for a while, and he was hoping no one would take on the cottage and the baking so he could make an offer for it.' He paused, wondering if he'd caused her to be upset. 'I'm sorry. I thought you knew.' He glanced at Minnie, and all she could do was bite her lip and glare at him.

Abby smiled tightly. 'No, I wasn't aware of that.'

CHAPTER TWO

Abby didn't blame Gordon. He was straightforward. Euan was the sneaky one. Then there was Minnie, but from the look on her face she'd been roped into Euan's plan without really intending any harm.

Minnie looked embarrassed. 'I apologise for any upset, Abby.' Her apology was sincere and she wished she'd never let Euan borrow Bracken.

'It's okay, Minnie. I assume Euan got you involved in his plan and I'd rather not have any bad feelings between us because of him.' The last thing she needed was awkwardness with Minnie, due to Euan's interference, especially as she intended doing business with her.

Minnie was eager to agree. 'I hope we can start again, and you'll still come along to the quilting bee tonight.'

Abby nodded. 'I will.' She hadn't pinned her hopes on a fresh start in a lovely cottage by the sea to have things dashed because of Euan's stupid antics. And she was excited to become part of the local quilting bee. This was a bonus she hadn't anticipated — a group of quilters right on her doorstep. They'd be able to share patterns and techniques and chat about quilting, something she'd often wanted to do. No, she wasn't going to miss out on that.

Gordon sighed and wasn't sure what to say.

Abby looked at him. 'And I don't blame you, Gordon.'

He tried to smile, but inwardly he was kicking himself for mentioning about Euan wanting the cottage.

'A clean slate then for all of us,' said Minnie.

'Yes,' Abby said firmly, wanting no more to do with Euan's underhanded tactics.

With the atmosphere in the shop now feeling lighter, Minnie started to pick the items from the shelves that Abby needed for her baking, and put them on the counter. The grocery shop was well stocked with bags of flour, yeast, sugar, dried fruit, cocoa powder, syrup, treacle and extracts such as vanilla.

'I'll order in sprinkles and a few other things for you,' Minnie said to Abby.

'I only popped in for the jam,' said Gordon, 'so now that Abby's baking the cakes I'll be going. See you both tonight.' He smiled and left Abby and Minnie to get on with the shopping.

'Gordon's lovely,' Minnie confided moments after he left. 'He's single, and does quite well for himself with his tea shop. He bought over the business a few years ago when the previous owners retired. We thought he was going to modernise it, and in some ways he has, especially the kitchen, installing new ovens and other gadgets, but at the hub of it he's kept the original elements and vintage decor. It's like stepping into the past while still feeling fresh — a lovely place for our quilting bee.'

'It sounds great. I love vintage decor.'

'What sort of quilts do you sew?' Minnie asked. 'I prefer traditional patterns, but I've been thinking of making a modern quilt. One or two of our members have veered towards that style.'

'I've sewn various types. I also like to mix both styles, traditional and modern,' said Abby.

'I think you'll enjoy the atmosphere at our wee bee. Of course, we chat about quilting, but we share gossip and giggles and it's always a fun night. Gordon's a great cook and lays on a nice selection of cakes, scones and flans for our evening tea. He trained as a chef in the city, in Glasgow, and moved here when he bought the tea shop. And as I say, he's single and very nice.'

Abby smiled to herself and began picking items from the shelves, things she needed to stock her kitchen cupboards including tea, coffee, sugar, sea salt, herbs, spices and various condiments. 'I'm single, but I'm not looking for romance, not yet anyway. I want to get settled in, get the baking up and running.'

'I've been on my own since my husband passed a few years ago. My shop keeps me busy and I enjoy the quilting bee.'

'No single men you're interested in?'

'Well, there's one, Shawn, he's a farmer, but I'm too set in my ways to start dating. I like my life the way it is right now. But a pretty young woman like you well...there are a few eligible men. There's Euan...'

Abby's expression vetoed that choice.

'He's obviously in your bad books, but he's not usually the sneaky sort. I'm sure it's bothering him not being honest with you.'

14

'Why does he want the cottage? Surely he's got his field and I saw a house on it.' It was a stone–built, two storey house. Abby preferred her cosy cottage, but why would a man like Euan want it when he already had a home?

'His grandfather owned several fields in the area, and built the cottage you're in. Euan is wealthy, and although his grandfather sold off most of the fields and the cottage, Euan still works the land, the three fields he has left, and has always wanted to own the bakery cottage. He grew up in it and hoped he could buy it.' She shrugged. 'Josh's firm was handling the legal side of dealing with the cottage. Apparently Euan had made his interest clear to Josh, but then we heard that you'd accepted the offer. I don't know the details. Josh keeps his business matters private, especially from me as I'm tagged as being a bit of a tittle–tattle.'

Abby smiled. 'I expected that everyone in a small community like this would know each other's business.'

'Yes, we do. I like to think of it as taking an interest in your neighbours. Josh prefers to keep things private, and that's fine for his type of business. He keeps himself to himself most of the time. I don't know him very well. He's away a lot working in the city, stocks and shares and all that.'

'I've only dealt with him via my solicitor. I haven't spoken to him myself.'

'He lives in the mansion higher up on the hills overlooking the bay. His father remarried a few years ago and moved to London and gave the property to Josh. A beautiful house. It's hidden by the trees so you probably haven't seen it.'

'No, I don't think I have.' Abby was sure she hadn't seen a mansion on her drive down to the coast.

'Josh is another single man, at least according to his housekeeper. You'll meet her at the quilting bee, but he insists she doesn't talk about his private business. I think that's right though.' She smiled at Abby. 'Josh is very rich and very handsome, if a bit elusive, but some women like a man with a touch of mystery about him.'

'Not me. I've had years of working with, dealing with and dating men with all sorts of agendas and I'd prefer someone straightforward. Game playing is so tiring.'

'I know what you mean. I always knew where I stood with my husband, and it's what I loved most about him. Good looks can fade, but trust and loyalty are enduring.'

A wave of emotion washed over Abby and she blinked away the tears that threatened to spill out. She smiled and hoped Minnie hadn't noticed as they continued to pick items from the shelves.

Minnie lowered her tone. 'Did I say something out of turn?'

'No,' Abby was quick to assure her. 'I just...I've not had a lot of luck when it comes to men and trust and loyalty. To tell you the truth, I think there's something about me that makes them feel they can mess me about.' She took a steadying breath. 'I think I've been so anxious to leave the past behind and make a fresh start here and the first thing that happens is...' She broke off and concentrated on reading her grocery list.

'Euan being underhanded?'

Abby nodded. 'And wanting my cottage when I've only just moved in. It feels like an intrusion right from the start. I guess I pictured things differently. More like this, chatting to people and settling in. Now I'm going to be looking over my shoulder wondering if Euan is trying to find a way to get his hands on my cottage. Maybe he'll make an offer to Josh and between them they'll thwart me.'

Minnie put the large bag of flour she was holding on the counter. 'No, no, that won't happen. The cottage is yours, and Euan isn't usually so sneaky. And Josh, well, he's not the type that Euan could persuade to do anything underhanded.'

Abby took a deep breath. 'Sorry, you're right. I'm excited to be here. I'm on my own, and that's okay, but I'm so used to having to fight for my corner in the advertising world. I guess I need to unwind and get into the easy pace of life here.'

'Starting with baking cakes and then attending the quilting bee.'

'Yes, ease myself in real slow.' Abby smiled. 'I'm hoping I can make some sort of living from the baking, but I honestly don't see how Netta made much money.'

'She didn't. It was enough to tick over on. She owned the cottage and lived off the money her husband left her. She loved her baking and it was more of a hobby that brought in a small profit.' Minnie frowned. 'You'll probably have to work on a sideline business if you want to earn a decent living. I don't know your circumstances, but I assume you made a fair amount from your job in advertising.'

'I did, and I have savings, however...' She shrugged. 'This is going to be a challenge, but I've always wanted to live by the sea, and maybe open my own quilt shop.'

Minnie's eyes lit up with glee. 'A quilt shop?'

'Or a quilting business. Perhaps I could have a baking and quilting cottage. Surely that wouldn't be breaking the terms of the agreement.'

'I wouldn't think so. You should ask Josh. He'll keep you right on those matters.'

'Yes, I'll do that.' Abby felt excited at the prospect of getting a little quilt business up and running alongside the baking.

Other customers came into the shop and Abby paid for her items. There was quite a load of groceries for her to carry.

'I'll order the other things for you and they should be here tomorrow or the day after,' said Minnie. 'Are you sure you can manage to carry everything?'

'I brought the car. Thanks for your help, Minnie, and I'll see you tonight.' Abby started to carry the groceries outside to her car, and passed a strapping farmer, a mature man, big and strong, going in loaded with a delivery of fresh eggs from his farm.

When Abby went back into the shop to pick up the last of her items, she saw Minnie chatting happily to the farmer and sensed a connection between them. She mouthed to Minnie — *is that Shawn*?

Minnie secretly nodded to Abby, and they exchanged a knowing smile.

Abby gave her the thumbs up. *Very nice.*

Minnie giggled and then continued to deal with the farmer's delivery.

Abby loaded the groceries into the back seat of her car and drove the short distance to her cottage.

As she was taking her bags inside, she saw Euan striding across his field again. He was heading straight for her.

Abby dumped the groceries down, marched to the edge of her garden and called out to him. 'I'm not selling my cottage, Euan.' She sounded determined.

Euan stopped and stood where he was. She saw the tension in his expression as he realised she knew his intentions. He tried to hide

17

how hard this hit him, but there was no disguising the mix of disappointment and anger at his own stupidity. He nodded at Abby. Message received. They both knew where they stood.

Euan's heart thundered in his chest and his opinion of himself diminished. What a fool he'd made of himself. Abby had every right to be upset with him, though he hadn't expected her to be so forthright.

It was only when he walked away that she noticed the bunch of flowers he was holding, freshly picked from his field and tied with straw ribbons. They dangled from his hand as if they weighed a ton as he trudged back up the field to his own house.

Abby made a start on the baking and tried not to think about the retreating figure of Euan or the bunch of flowers she assumed were for her.

She prepared the baking tins and preheated one of the ovens. The cooker was much more user friendly than she'd anticipated considering what a monster it was taking up a large slice of the kitchen.

She followed Netta's exact recipe even though it was a simple Victoria sponge and she'd made those lots of times for herself.

The mixer was a dream, and everything in the kitchen worked so well being a blend of vintage stalwarts and new items. The cupboards were quite well stocked now with grocery items and it was starting to feel like home.

There was a view of the garden from the kitchen window, and pretty floral curtains were draped up with ribbons and matched the cushion covers on the chairs.

While the cakes were baking, she relaxed on one of the kitchen chairs, gazing out at the garden, sipping a cup of tea and thinking how wonderful it was to be living in a cottage like this. She'd cut a thick slice of crusty bread and spread it with Minnie's raspberry jam. It tasted tangy and delicious and would be perfect for the sponge filling.

She hadn't eaten a proper meal all day, and now with it being so close to going to the quilting bee, she didn't want to spoil her appetite for the food at the tea shop.

When the cakes were cooked to a light golden brown, she let them cool before adding the raspberry jam and buttercream. They'd turned out really well and she put them aside to take to the tea shop later.

She then set about making her bed with the clean linen so it would be ready to flop into after her night out. She put one of her favourite quilts on top. It was a floral quilt she'd designed using a selection of pretty fabrics including bluebell and cornflower prints and it suited the flowery theme of the cottage. The old–fashioned chest of drawers in the bedroom and the dressing table had been painted eggshell blue and this matched the blue tones of her quilt.

With the time flying in, she decided to shower and get ready for the evening ahead.

She towel dried her hair and let it dry naturally, brushing it smooth and silky. Raking through her clothes, she decided to wear jeans and a blue top and kept her makeup light and natural looking.

She folded one of her floral design quilts and put it in a bag along with a sewing kit and thread. Minnie had said that there were plenty of items to share at the quilting bee and she was looking forward to seeing what the other members were making.

With the cakes packed safety in a bag, she put a white cardigan on, picked up the quilt bag and walked along the shore to the tea shop. The sea glistened in the evening light and the air was quite warm. The scent of the grass and fields along the shoreline mingled with the sea air, and she enjoyed the walk itself, so different from being in the city. It was calm and quiet with only a few people around, mainly near the shops. The lights from the shops glowed in the twilight and twinkle lights were draped along part of the shore's esplanade. Most of the shops were closed for the night, making the tea shop and the bar restaurant stand out with their bright lights, creating a welcoming atmosphere, and making her glad she'd decided to venture out on her first evening here.

As she gazed out at the sparkling sea, she saw lights far in the distance along the bay, hinting that another small town or village was perched on the coast. She was so busy looking at the view that she stumbled slightly on a rut in the grass and dropped her quilt bag. Trying not to drop the cakes, she bent down to pick up the quilt bag, and it was then that she was aware of a man running towards her. The same man she'd seen running earlier. The handsome shadow.

Within seconds he was right there beside her, having thought she'd taken a tumble.

19

'Let me help you,' he said, picking up the quilt bag as she reached down for it. His hand accidentally brushed against hers and sent a rush of excitement through her. This man was handsome, tall and very fit by the looks of him. Maybe he was a boxer or some sort of fighter. He had an intense look to him. His dark hair was swept back from his face and he'd gained a light golden tan from running outdoors. But his sculptured features bore no hint of being a brawler, so perhaps she was mistaken. He wore charcoal grey training trousers with a black T–shirt that emphasised his broad shoulders, lean torso and strong arms. His eyes were a fascinating pale grey with dark lashes, and he gazed at her, checking to see if she was all right.

'Are you okay?' He handed the bag to her. His voice was rich and deep and washed over her in the evening air.

'Yes, thank you.' Apart from her heart racing as the instant attraction hit her without warning. To be fair, quite a few women would find a man like him a pleasant distraction. She tried not to look at the lean muscles in his arms as he helped her with the bag. And unless she was mistaken there was a six pack under that tight T–shirt of his that made her want to reach out and touch it. This was not something she'd ever done, or intended to do, but the thought of it was sparking in her mind, tempting her. Oh yes, this man was a walking temptation. She stepped back and forced what she hoped was a casual smile.

'I'm fine. I wasn't looking where I was going.' She tried to sound calm when she felt the complete opposite.

He glanced around. 'It's getting dark. If you don't mind me asking, where are you going? It's safe around here, but still...a woman on her own, especially as you're new here. I'd be happy to walk with you.'

What. An. Offer.

Abby took a deep breath. He'd never know how tempted she was to accept his offer, but unfortunate past experiences with good looking guys had left her wary of becoming involved with them. Men like him were nice to look at, but the last thing she needed was another broken heart. Nope. No way was she venturing down that route again. Not that she thought he was chatting her up. Definitely not. He gave no hint of this. Besides, a man like him was probably taken, and a woman like her with her quaint quilting and cakes was hardly his type. Despite her career in advertising, she was a homebody at heart, and he seemed like a man who led an adventurous life.

'I'm going to the quilting bee at the tea shop,' she said, motioning to where it was nearby. 'But thanks for the offer...' she trailed off, not knowing his name and not sure that she wanted to. Hopefully he'd run on and disappear wherever he was going.

'Josh,' he said.

'*You're Josh*?' If she hadn't been so surprised she could've hidden her reaction better.

'Yes. You must be Abby.'

She was nodding while her heart beat faster. *This was Josh?* Somehow she'd imagined him to be a mature man, wearing a suit, sitting at his desk being businesslike, not packing abs, leanly muscled and in his mid thirties, barely older than she was.

'I spoke to your solicitor regarding the cottage,' he elaborated. 'I saw you moving in. Is the cottage to your liking?'

'It is. It's lovely. I love it.' She paused, not sure what else to say to him. Everything about him, from their chance encounter to those lean muscles of his, threw her senses haywire.

'It's a nice cottage,' he said. 'And so handy being right by the sea.'

'Yes, perfect for taking an early morning dip. No excuses now for not keeping fit. Just jump out of bed and run down to the sea and dive in.' She paused, hearing herself babble nervously. 'With my clothes on, not right out of bed with nothing on, not that I sleep starkers or go commando...' Shut up, she mentally scolded herself as her cheeks burned fiery pink. 'What I mean is, wearing a swimsuit.'

He pressed his firm lips together and had the manners to suppress the smirk that was threatening to form. He hadn't smiled at her yet, and that intense expression of his cast a brooding shadow across his handsome features. But he was secretly smiling at her, oh yes he was, and she didn't blame him. What a stupid thing to say. Come on, she urged herself, change the subject to something else to...*anything*.

'You live in the mansion on the hill,' she said, remembering what Minnie had told her.

'I do.' He pointed up to it, and she noticed a large house, far up on the hill. The windows were lit up and that's the only reason she would've known it was there as it was hidden so well by the trees.

Her heart wouldn't calm down just being near him, so she smiled politely and said, 'Well, I'd better get going. I don't want to be late.'

He nodded. 'Enjoy your evening at the quilting bee.'

'I will.'

He walked away and that's when she remembered something and called out to him. 'Would it be okay if I ran a little quilting business from the cottage as well as baking?'

He paused and looked round at her.

'Would it infringe the agreement?'

He frowned. 'I wouldn't think it would affect it, but I'll check and let you know. I have your phone number.'

'Thanks.'

She walked away, eager to breathe and let her burning cheeks cool down. However, moments later she was aware that he'd run to catch up with her.

'What type of quilting business?' he said.

'Sewing and designing quilts.' She opened the bag. 'Quilts like this.'

He admired her handiwork. 'You made this yourself?'

'Yes.'

'I thought you worked in advertising.' His pale grey eyes gave her a questioning glance. They had a quicksilver quality rather like the surface of the sea.

'I did, but I've always loved quilting and sewing, and of course baking. I made a good living in the city at the ad agency, however it's doubtful I could make adequate money solely from baking at the cottage.'

'And you think you could run a quilting business here?' He wasn't doubting her, just making sure he understood.

'Yes. I'd sell them online, create a website, advertise them properly.'

'Your advertising experience would certainly be handy.' He looked right at her. 'I can't think of any reason why it would affect the agreement, but I'll check and call you tomorrow.'

And then he ran off, leaving her to walk the short distance to the tea shop with her mind whirling due to the effect he'd had on her.

She was sure she was still blushing because she could feel her cheeks burning and didn't want the ladies to see her like this, especially as someone might have noticed her talking to Josh.

She paused for a moment to calm down when a man's voice spoke over her shoulder.

'Did you bring the cakes with you?'

She looked round to find Gordon smiling at her. He'd been handing in the cheese and onion flans he'd cooked for the bar restaurant. The sleeves of his white shirt were rolled up and it was unbuttoned at the neck. He looked good. He was one of those men she felt comfortable with. There was a warmth about him that made her feel at ease.

'Yes, two Victoria sponge cakes as promised.' She handed them to him.

'Great, let's go in. The bee started a bit early tonight and they're looking forward to meeting you.'

The tea shop windows were aglow and Abby could hear the chatter as they approached. The exterior was traditional with a vintage facia, scalloped canopy and flower baskets hanging outside. A sandwich board listed the day's special menu items including Scottish cheddar flans, fresh fruit tarts, and buttermilk scones with cream and jam.

Gordon opened the door for her. 'Everything okay?' he whispered quickly.

She blinked at him.

'You seem a bit flushed. Maybe it's all the sea air and sunshine.'

'Definitely,' Abby lied, and followed him inside the tea shop.

CHAPTER THREE

The quilting bee was a hive of activity. The members, all ladies, were busy chatting and sitting in the hub at the rear of the tea shop, an extension that led on to a garden at the back. The patio doors were open to allow the air to waft in, and everyone was seated at tables piled with all types of quilts and fabric.

The tables were used for buffet functions and could be assembled for evenings like this and then folded away. The women were sitting sewing and sharing gossip. Abby wondered if she was one of the topics of the evening. Gordon had said that the bee had started early and she knew she wasn't late, so perhaps they wanted to discuss her before she arrived.

She noticed a few of them were doing English paper piecing, while others were fussy cutting fabric or hand stitching binding.

Sewing machines were set up and a couple of women were using them to sew their quilts. The ladies were all so busy they hadn't noticed her yet, so before joining the bee, she paused and looked around.

The tea shop had several customers seated at small tables near the front windows with a view of the sea. It was a lovely shop and Gordon had kept a lot of the original decor. The tiles around the fireplace were floral and cream, and although the fire wasn't lit due to the warmer weather, it was set ready to light if needed.

The shop's lighting created a cosy but bright atmosphere. Vintage lamps with glass shades, some coloured pink and amber, gave a glow to parts of the tea shop while other areas were brightly lit such as the main counter and cabinets.

Abby hadn't expected to find such an array of cakes, scones and sweets on offer. One of the glass cabinets contained delicious fruit tarts filled with strawberries, blackberries, blueberries and peaches glazed with apricot jam. Another was stocked with sweets — chocolates, truffles, butterscotch, toffee, Scottish tablet and fudge cut into squares that could be purchased by the piece, allowing customers to enjoy a selection of different flavours of fudge from vanilla to caramel.

Gordon put Abby's cakes down on the counter. 'These look delicious. I'll slice them and bring them through later for the tea break.'

'This is a beautiful shop, Gordon,' said Abby, looking around her. The aroma of coffee mingled with the scent of the bakery products, and she noticed on the menu board a list of savoury treats such as onion flan, sandwiches, cheese pastries, Scotch broth and lentil soup. Her tummy rumbled, but there was so much chatter from the ladies that no one heard.

Gordon smiled at her. 'Thank you.' He wished he had time to chat to her, but the quilting bee evenings were always so busy.

Stairs led up to the second floor. 'Are there tables upstairs as well?' she asked, wondering if the business extended to two levels.

'No, I live above the tea shop. Home and work together, very handy.'

'Yes, I'm sure it is.'

'I'll give you a tour of the premises when the happy chaos subsides,' he said.

He was concentrating on packing a white cardboard sweet box with individual pieces of fudge, tablet, butterscotch and chocolate truffles. Each piece was a little temptation in itself and she didn't want to disturb him as he made up the order, so she went through to the back of the tea shop where the women were sewing.

'Abby!' Minnie called to her. 'Come away in.'

The warm smiles and cheerfulness from the ladies made Abby feel genuinely welcome.

'I've been telling the ladies about you moving into Netta's cottage and that you'll be doing the baking like before,' Minnie said to Abby.

Abby nodded and smiled, feeling slightly overwhelmed by the welcome.

'If there's anything you need for the cottage let me know,' one of the women said to Abby. The woman was in her fifties with a flurry of light auburn hair and was sewing a quilt as she spoke. 'I wasn't sure when you were arriving or I'd have stocked your fridge with milk and fresh groceries.'

'This is Pearl,' said Minnie, introducing her to Abby. 'She's Josh's housekeeper.'

'Thank you, Pearl, but everything is ideal at the cottage,' Abby told her.

'Are you settling in okay?' Pearl asked.

'I'm settling in fine. It's a lovely cottage and I like the garden too.'

'Did you bake the Victoria sponges for Gordon?' said Minnie.

'Yes, I managed to figure out how to use the cooker,' Abby explained. 'It doesn't seem to have any foibles and the oven baked the cakes great. I used Netta's recipe.'

'I loved her chocolate cakes,' one of the ladies commented. She was similar in age to Minnie and Pearl with light blonde hair. 'I'm Judy by the way.'

'Pleased to meet you,' Abby acknowledged. 'I'm planning on making the chocolate cakes.'

This claim was met with several of the ladies nodding enthusiastically.

'Judy and her husband own the bar restaurant next door,' Minnie said to Abby.

'Let me know how to place an order with you for the cakes and the special shortbread,' said Judy, smiling at Abby. 'Our customers always enjoyed the shortbread. I'll buy a few big tins of it if you'll make them.'

'I'd be happy to do that for you, Judy,' Abby confirmed.

Further introductions were made, and Abby was seated between Pearl and Minnie. Pearl was hand stitching the binding on to a quilt.

'I'll tell Josh you're happy with things at the cottage,' Pearl said to Abby.

'I told him I loved the cottage.'

Pearl paused mid stitch. 'I didn't realise you'd spoken to him.'

'I met him on the way here tonight. I stumbled, dropped my quilt bag and Josh came running and helped me pick it up. He even offered to walk with me to the tea shop to see that I was safe. He seems very nice.'

The chatter faded to a fascinated silence.

'Are you sure it was Josh you spoke to?' said Minnie.

Abby nodded. 'He introduced himself. He was tall with dark hair and very handsome. He'd been running along the shore.'

Judy stared at Abby in disbelief, then tried to contain her reaction. 'Sorry, it's just that Josh is...well, he's a heartbreaker, isn't he, ladies?'

'He certainly is,' said Minnie as the others nodded in unanimous agreement.

'Josh is very fit,' Pearl commented.

'I didn't know it was him when he ran over to me,' Abby told them. 'I thought at first he looked like a boxer or some sort of fighter.'

'Oh, he is,' said Pearl. 'But he doesn't like me talking about him.'

Minnie was keen to find out more details from Abby. 'So did Josh just come running up to you when he saw you stumble?'

'He did. He said he'd seen me moving into the cottage, so he knew who I was.'

Minnie was really intrigued. 'And he offered to walk with you to the tea shop tonight?'

'Yes, why? Is there something I should know about him?' Abby asked her.

Minnie, Pearl, Judy and several other women glanced at each other.

'It's just that, as I said to you earlier, Josh keeps himself to himself. I'm not saying that if you were dangling off the edge of a cliff Josh wouldn't come to your assistance, but if you'd only dropped your quilt bag well...' Minnie's words trailed off, leaving a tone of insinuation that this was not regular behaviour from Josh.

'Maybe he's got a fancy for you?' Judy suggested to Abby.

'I don't think so.' Abby started to blush bright pink.

Judy wasn't convinced. 'It's not like Josh to be so friendly.'

'He can seem standoffish,' said Pearl, 'but deep down he's very thoughtful.'

Judy persisted with her theory. 'You all know what I mean. Josh is the mysterious, brooding type. Now if it had been Gordon, I'd have expected him to offer to help and walk Abby to the quilting bee. Or even Euan. But Josh?' She shrugged.

Abby frowned, wondering what to make of this.

'All we're saying is, it's a wee bit out of character for Josh,' Minnie explained.

Judy smiled. 'Perhaps we've got a new romance sparking?'

Abby was quick to quash such a suggestion before it became a rumour around the small community. 'No, definitely not. Josh was just being polite.'

The looks they gave Abby were edged with knowing smiles.

Abby found herself starting to smile too. 'There's no romance,' she insisted.

Minnie grinned at Abby. 'Not yet, but it could be brewing.'

'I'm not interested in romance at the moment. I'm far too busy,' Abby told them. 'I want to concentrate on settling in, baking the cakes and starting up a quilting business.' She looked at Minnie. 'I asked Josh if this would be okay.'

'What did he say?' said Minnie.

'He said he didn't think it infringed the agreement I made when I accepted the cottage, but he's going to check and let me know.'

'This sounds promising,' said Minnie. 'I know that Pearl doesn't like to talk about Josh's private life, and that's fine, but we can talk about him. And if he was running after you along the shore tonight, I think Josh could be interested in you, Abby.' Minnie sounded enthusiastic. 'Maybe Josh will ask you out on a date.'

Gordon walked into the full effect of their suggestion. He was carrying a tray of cakes, including slices of Abby's Victoria sponges. He stopped as if the comment hit him hard.

Gordon frowned at Abby. 'Josh has asked you out?' He'd misheard their conversation, but his reaction created further nudges and knowing looks from the ladies. Gordon sounded jealous. This could only mean that he was interested in Abby.

Abby shook her head at Gordon. 'No, Josh hasn't asked me out.' She explained what had happened.

Even Gordon was inclined to agree with the women when he heard the details. 'Josh must like you, Abby. If he saw you moving in, he'll have realised you're lovely.'

The women stared at Gordon.

'What I mean is...'

Minnie smiled. 'I think we know fine what you mean, Gordon.'

Embarrassed and knowing he'd never gain the upper hand against the quilting bee ladies, Gordon put the cake tray down on a table and retreated back through to the front of the tea shop, muttering something about bringing them their scones with cream and jam.

Abby felt the colour rise in her cheeks.

Minnie placed a calming hand on her arm. 'Oh, don't worry. There's always interest when a newcomer arrives.'

'But it's so out of character for Josh,' said Judy, continuing to stir up the romantic speculation.

'It certainly is,' Minnie agreed.

Pearl nudged Abby. 'Gordon's definitely taken with you.'

Abby tried to hide her blushes, and pulled her quilt out of her bag. 'I brought this with me. I've almost finished it.'

Her distraction worked and the focus fell on Abby's floral quilt.

'This is beautiful work,' Minnie complimented her, reaching out to lightly touch the top stitching. 'I see you've hand stitched it.'

'Yes, I did. Sometimes I machine stitch my quilts, but I enjoy hand stitching too. It depends on the design. Sitting on the couch and hand stitching can be so relaxing.'

Minnie agreed. 'It is. I'm like you, I do both.'

The other ladies were keen to look at Abby's handiwork.

'How long did this take you?' asked Pearl.

Abby wasn't sure. 'I tend to work on several quilt projects at a time. I like making large quilts and mini quilts, so it varies. Lately, I've been so busy getting things ready to move here that I haven't had time to finish them.'

Judy admired Abby's design. 'Is this your own design?'

'Yes,' said Abby. 'I like creating my own patterns and designed this with a floral theme. And I love adding appliqué.' Abby had sewn floral appliqué on to the quilt. 'I'm hoping to run a quilt business from the cottage as well as baking.'

Several women came over to study the quilt. Most of the members were experienced quilters and appreciated her skill.

'What type of thread did you use for the top stitching?' Judy asked.

'It's a variegated cotton thread in shades of blue.' Abby pointed to the stitching. 'The different tones of blue from pastel to turquoise and deep sea blues blend with the fabric and enhance the overall design.'

Judy studied the thread work. 'I haven't used a variegated thread before on my quilts, but seeing this I'm going to try it.'

'I mainly use grey thread as it blends with all colours of fabric and sinks into the design,' said Minnie. 'However, I want to try a variegated thread now. It would make a nice change.'

'Grey is what I used to stitch with, then I found a variegated grey thread and I liked it,' said Abby. 'Later, I tried out variegated blue and pink tones and I've been stitching with those threads for a while.'

Minnie was thoughtful. 'A mix of grey tones sounds interesting. I'll get some of that as well as the blue.'

'I'm popping into the town tomorrow. I could pick up the thread we need from the fabric shop,' Pearl offered.

Minnie, Judy and a few others told Pearl what they'd like her to buy.

Abby had the thread with her and showed them the exact colours she used. Pearl noted these.

They were still talking about thread when Gordon came through with a trolley laden with cakes, savoury pastries and scones. Then he brought the tea through.

The ladies stopped sewing and got ready to enjoy their tea break.

Abby was glad that they didn't tease Gordon about what he'd said earlier, and the evening settled into discussing quilting.

'Did you have a quilt business in the city?' one of the ladies asked Abby.

'No, but I've always wanted to have my own quilt shop. I've sold some of my quilts in the past. Do any of you sell your quilts?'

'Not really,' said Minnie. 'We love quilting, but don't sell the things we make. I fold mine up and keep them in my sewing cupboard.'

'We sometimes contribute items to the local fetes and summer stalls during the fair,' Pearl added. 'But I stash most of my quilts along with my fabric.'

'I keep mine or give them to friends and family,' said Judy. 'I have a wardrobe full of finished quilts and my fabric stash.'

'Are you going to advertise your quilts?' Minnie asked Abby. 'With your background in advertising you'll know how to do this.'

Abby nodded. 'Yes, I'm going to set up a website and sell them online.'

'I admire your ambition, Abby,' said Pearl. 'I wouldn't know where to start.'

Several of the women nodded in agreement.

'There's a woman who sells hand dyed yarn from her cottage,' said Minnie. 'She has a website and sells her knitted items on there as well.'

This comment sparked further interest from the bee members, especially as Abby admired their quilts and offered encouragement to them.

'Your quilts are lovely,' said Abby. 'I think people would buy them if you targeted them in the right way to potential customers.' She stopped when she heard herself sounding like she still worked in advertising, but the spark had been ignited and now a few interested faces were looking to her for advice.

'Maybe the best idea would be to combine your efforts,' said Abby. 'Set up a website for the quilting bee members to sell your quilts. This would allow you to see if there was enough interest from customers to make it worth your while, and you could back each other up. As you've already established the quilting bee and know each other well, it's something that could add a bit extra money and fun to your bee.'

'I update the website for our bar restaurant,' said Judy. 'I'd need a hand setting up a website for the quilting bee, but I'd be happy to keep it updated with quilts for sale.'

'I'd help you set it up, Judy,' Abby offered. 'It doesn't have to be complicated, just visually enticing with beautiful pictures of the quilts and descriptions of each product.'

The details of how they'd go about this were discussed enthusiastically as they enjoyed their tea break, and by the time Gordon came through to clear away the cups and plates, they were buzzing with excitement.

'We're planning to go into business,' Minnie told him. 'What do you think?'

Gordon looked at Abby, not blaming her, but knowing she had something to do with it. He was used to the ladies sewing and gossiping, but talking about setting up a quilting bee business was something else.

'It sounds promising,' he said. 'Your quilts are beautiful. I think people would want to buy them.'

Minnie was bubbling with enthusiasm. 'Abby wants us to take photos of our quilts, and we were wondering if we could snap a few pictures in your tea shop to create an attractive setting?'

'You're welcome to photograph them here,' Gordon confirmed. 'I can set up a table with afternoon tea or whatever you'd like to have in your pictures. Do you want to take some tonight or during the day?'

'We need to decide what quilts we're selling,' said Minnie, 'then we could arrange a suitable time with you.'

'Fine, just let me know,' Gordon replied cheerfully. He cast another glance at Abby. 'Will you be photographing your quilts here too?'

'I wouldn't mind,' Abby told him. 'You have so many pretty vintage items in your shop. It would be an ideal background for photos.'

Gordon started to suggest ideas for the backgrounds, including using his cakes, and setting up a cosy scene by the fire.

While they were talking about taking photographs, Abby's phone rang.

'Hello...hi, Josh,' Abby said, causing the women and Gordon to become quiet and stare at her.

Minnie mouthed to Abby. *Is Josh phoning you*?

Abby nodded to Minnie and continued to talk to Josh. She was as surprised as everyone else to hear from him. The sound of his deep voice sent a rush of excitement through her, and she tried to hide this behind an air of cheerful chatter.

'I thought you'd like to know while you're still at the quilting bee that it's okay to run a quilt business from the cottage,' said Josh.

'That's great. I was just discussing selling my quilts and taking photos of them in Gordon's tea shop.'

'I'll draw up a letter confirming your use of the cottage for a quilting business,' said Josh. 'I can drop it off to you, or perhaps you'd like to come up to the house tomorrow and pick it up yourself.'

Josh's offer hung in the air for a second as Abby considered what to do.

'I expect you'll be busy baking during the morning,' Josh added, 'but if you're not busy tomorrow afternoon, come up for tea and sign the letter here. Bring any quilts you'd like to take photographs of too. The house has plenty of backgrounds you could use.'

'Eh, yes, I'll drop by your house in the afternoon,' Abby confirmed, trying not to smile when she saw the reaction to this on the women's faces. And Gordon's reaction too. He was as surprised as any of them.

'Shall we say around two–thirty?' Josh suggested.

'Yes, I'll see you then.' Abby's heart fluttered with excitement as she clicked her phone off.

There was a second of stunned silence after the call and then Abby told them the details.

'Josh says I can use the cottage for a quilting business and he's putting it in writing for me. He's invited up to his house to sign the letter...and have tea with him — and take photos of my quilts.'

Minnie's eyes were wide with wonder. 'At his house? Josh has invited you to tea?'

'He has,' Abby replied, trying to suppress her excitement.

Pearl blinked as if this information didn't quite sink in. 'Josh doesn't invite many people to his house. He meets them elsewhere for business, to sign documents, discuss deals, stuff like that.'

'Perhaps he thinks it'll save time if I pop up and deal with the business letter,' said Abby.

Pearl shook her head. 'No, Josh's house is his castle. He's making a play for you.'

Judy nodded. 'Oh yes, Josh is going to ask you out on a date. This is a very handy excuse to get you up to his house. He's trying to impress you.'

Abby didn't like to tell them that Josh had impressed her. He was incredibly handsome, successful and had a good reputation according to her solicitor. She wanted to see his house. A mansion overlooking the sea sounded brilliant. There were worse things than having afternoon tea with a man like Josh.

'Abby's a city girl,' said Minnie. 'She's not easily impressed, especially with her background in the advertising business.' She looked to Abby to confirm this.

'That's true,' replied Abby.

'I'm sure you've met lots of high–powered, rich businessmen in your time,' Minnie added.

'I have, and I'm used to dealing with them,' Abby assured her. Though to be fair, none of them were in Josh's league when it came to being handsome.

This remark made Gordon take a defensive stance. 'Josh hardly knows you, Abby. You could meet him here at my tea shop and sign the letter.'

'Josh would never do anything improper,' Pearl told Gordon and then smiled at Abby. 'You should go to his house for tea.'

Minnie beamed with enthusiasm. 'Yes, and then tell us all the details.'

Gordon shook his head in dismay and looked at Abby. 'This wee community thrives on gossip and mischief.'

'And romance,' Judy added. 'Don't forget about the romance.'

Gordon couldn't forget about that, especially as he felt he'd missed out on the chance to ask Abby to be his guest for tea. He liked her, and thought he'd get to know her and then possibly ask her out on a date. Now he'd been outdone and outshone by Josh.

'Do you still want to take pictures of your quilts here at my tea shop?' Gordon asked Abby.

'Yes, it's such a lovely setting,' said Abby.

'I'll give you a tour of the shop later, as promised.' He sounded hopeful. Maybe she wouldn't get along with Josh. He doubted they had anything in common.

Further plans were discussed by the ladies at the bee after the tea break, including designing a logo for their website.

Minnie smiled brightly. 'I never expected to be selling my quilts, but now I'm excited to get this started. I'm picturing what quilts I want to sell and what to write for my descriptions.'

Pearl frowned. 'I've no idea what to write.'

Abby advised them. 'Start with the basics. The size of the quilt. What type of fabric was used. Most of our quilts are cotton, but state this and what type of thread it was sewn with. Describe the colours, even though they can see these in the photos, people like to know the colours and anything special in the fabric prints such as flowers. Customers are more inclined to buy, in my experience, if they can read a clear but interesting description of the product.'

Pearl was still unsure. 'If I showed you the quilts I'd like to sell, would you maybe help me write the descriptions, just to give me an idea of what I should include?' she asked Abby.

34

'Yes, of course,' Abby assured her.

One of the members asked tentatively, 'Do you really think people will want to buy our quilts?'

Abby nodded. 'For the past year or so I've wanted to open my own shop, or sell my quilts online, and I've been studying the market, looking at the prices of quilts, what type of customers buy handmade items like this. I just never gave up my advertising job, and now that I'm here at the cottage, I'm going to put all my research into practise, and I'm happy to share that information with you.'

'Won't we be competing against each other?' Minnie asked, suddenly realising this could be true.

'No, the quilting bee website will stand on its own, and my quilting business will be separate. However, if we pull our skills together, especially helping each other with the photos, we'll all do well. There's no guarantee that it'll be a roaring success, but with the right advertising and marketing strategy, it'll work okay.'

Minnie sounded adamant. 'I'm willing to give it a go. If it fizzles out, fair enough, but I think it'll give the quilting bee an extra bit of buzz.'

Judy agreed. 'I love my quilting, but there's something exciting about sewing with a real purpose, not just for fun. I like the idea of selling my quilts. Even if it's only a few.'

'We can start by promoting our quilts online,' said Abby. 'I'm also thinking of contacting boutique hotels and asking them if they're interested in buying quilts. I know of other types of companies, such as interior design firms, that might be interested in us supplying them with original quilts, one–off pieces that they can use for their clients.' Then she asked, 'Are any of you on social media?'

'Yes,' said Judy. 'Quite a few of us.'

'Well then, there's a handy way to get the word out that your quilts are for sale,' said Abby.

Fired up and keen to get their quilting bee website up and running, they continued to make their plans while sewing for the remainder of the evening.

When it was time to go home, Gordon waylaid Abby. 'Have you got a moment to look round the tea shop?'

Abby smiled at him. 'Yes, I'd love to see it.'

As Judy was leaving she said to Abby, 'I'll speak to you tomorrow about setting up the website. Pop into the bar restaurant or give me a call.' They promised to chat the following day.

The quilting bee members bought cakes and sweets to take home for their families or for themselves as treats, so the tea shop cabinets were slightly less packed by the time they'd gone.

'I always do a great trade on the quilting bee nights,' Gordon said to Abby.

Minnie and Pearl were among the last to leave the tea shop as Gordon cleared the things away and folded the tables.

Pearl winked and smiled at Abby. 'Have a nice time with Gordon. Don't be getting up to any mischief.'

Gordon looked round at Pearl and Minnie. 'I'm simply showing Abby the tea shop.'

Minnie grinned at him. 'I'm sure you are.'

Giggling at each other, Minnie and Pearl left, giving Abby a cheery wave.

CHAPTER FOUR

When everyone had gone, Gordon showed Abby around the tea shop. They started with the kitchen. 'With you being into baking, you'll appreciate having extra ovens and work surfaces that have space for mixing the cakes, then cooling them, and an area for decorating.' He gestured around. 'It's a fair size kitchen.'

Abby did appreciate the layout. 'I like this. My cottage kitchen is bigger than I thought it would be, and it's handy when you're busy to have room to put things down easily.'

Gordon nodded. 'I've kept the old fashioned jelly making pans.' The pans were hanging on the wall, gleaming beside the array of new pots and skillets. 'I don't use them, but they're part of the original kitchen and I like that. I buy my jam locally from Minnie and other ladies.'

Abby walked around, admiring the traditional pottery jars and ceramic teapots. 'I love the way the modern items blend with the things from a bygone era.'

Gordon then led her through to the front of the tea shop.

'I wanted to talk to you about your cakes,' he said, gesturing to the main display cabinets. 'Could you bake the Victoria sponges on an ongoing basis? I'm so busy these days, and the sponges are always one of the most popular cakes. It would save me a lot of time if I could order them from you.'

'Yes, I'd be happy to do that.'

He agreed to set up a payment method with her, and then handed her the box of chocolates she'd seen him packing earlier.

'These are for you.'

She opened the box to see a delicious selection of sweets — everything from pieces of fudge to tasty tablet and chocolate delicacies.

'Oh, thank you, Gordon. But you didn't have to do that.'

'I didn't. It's a welcoming gift from the quilting bee ladies.'

'That was so sweet of them.'

'Speaking of sweet, try my new fudge.' He pointed to a piece of rich fudge that was half dipped in chocolate. 'I'm developing my confectionery range. I trained as a patisserie chef and considered specialising in chocolatier work, but then I bought the tea shop. So now I'm making the sweets part of the shop's menu.'

Abby lifted the piece of fudge and tasted it. 'This is gorgeous. It's so sweet and smooth.' Abby tried to figure out what he'd added to make it so delicious.

Gordon revealed some of the ingredients. 'Double cream and butter, and sea salt to balance out the sweetness.'

The fudge had the perfect melt in the mouth consistency and was tasty without being sickly sweet. 'This is the best I've tasted.'

Gordon smiled proudly. 'I'm thinking of selling it online. I have a website for the tea shop, nothing elaborate, just basic, but maybe you could help me with the advertising, the wording. I heard you advising the ladies.'

'Of course. I'd be glad to help.' Working for years in advertising had instilled in her an automatic response when she saw a new product, and her mind would start planning how to advertise it. It was a habit she thought would wane once she settled into the lifestyle here, but clearly her skills were useful in the community.

Abby closed the box of sweets before she was tempted to eat more of the fudge, especially the milk chocolate version, and pieces bursting with jewel–like bits of glacé cherries. Then there were the squares of butterscotch and tablet.

'I'll have a look at your website and see if I can come up with some ideas for you,' Abby told him.

Gordon had his laptop set up behind the main counter. He flicked it on. 'I was thinking of adding a heading for sweets that are available in the tea shop.' He showed her the website.

Abby studied it. 'Yes, this would work, especially if you listed each product with a really good picture of it.'

Gordon agreed. 'Do you think I should add better pictures of the tea shop?' He looked at his website as if it didn't quite come up to his expectations. 'As I say, it's basic.'

'It's okay, but new pics that show all the lovely aspects of the tea shop would make it better.' She motioned to the fireplace that wasn't even included in any of the photos. 'You should show the fire lit up, a cosy scene with buttered scones and jam, slices of cake and a pot of tea in one of the lovely ceramic teapots you use for customers. Create the type of look people expect from a tea shop.' She pointed to the lamps. 'Include a photo of that area over there, with the warm glow of the vintage lamps, and again include some food, maybe the flans or the display cabinet with the cakes or confectionery. It's such a pretty shop. You should show it to full advantage. And definitely add a picture of the exterior. The front of the tea shop with the hanging baskets and how near it is to the sea.'

Gordon's expression showed his excitement. 'Yes, you're right. I could do so much better to present the tea shop with new photos. Thanks, Abby. I'll start thinking what to do.'

'If you need any more ideas for the advertising on your website, I'd be happy to help.'

'Would you?' He sounded so enthusiastic.

Abby nodded and smiled at him.

'I bet you didn't think you'd be inveigled into all this advertising when you moved here.'

'Nope.' She grinned at him. 'But maybe it'll help ease me into the life here. A bit of my past merging with my present. I did like working in advertising, but I've always loved my quilting and anything crafty, and home baking.'

'A woman of many talents,' he complimented her.

'If I can be a master of one, I'll be happy. Two would be great.' She was thinking of quilting and baking, but Gordon had another suggestion.

'There are other businesses around here that would be interested in your advertising expertise. You could have that as a sideline to supplement your baking.'

'Maybe. Everything's happened so fast since I arrived, which is great because sometimes it suits me to be thrown in at the deep end. It pushes me to do better. I pictured I'd be relaxing by the fire in the cottage by now and getting ready for my first night here.'

'That's right, this will be your first night in the cottage.' He shook his head as if this had just dawned on him. 'You've fitted in here so well I almost feel like I know you already.'

She looked at him. 'I feel the same.'

'That's a good sign,' he said. 'It means you were meant to be here.'

She smiled and nodded. 'Yes, I think I am.' She couldn't remember the last time she'd felt so comfortable with people. Despite Euan's skulduggery, everyone else was a breath of fresh air in comparison to the game players she'd encountered in her recent past.

Gordon continued giving Abby the full tour of the tea shop, including showing her the new curtains and quilted cushions the quilting bee ladies had made.

'The ladies helped me select the flowery fabric and sewed these during a couple of their quilting bee nights here.'

'There's nothing quite like having things like this made specially for you.'

He reached over to where an oven glove was pinned up on the wall. 'And look at this. A quilted oven glove in the shape of a teapot.' The detailed stitching on it was lovely. 'Minnie made it for me. It's too nice to use so I pinned it up as part of the decor.'

Abby's thoughts immediately went to advertising. 'Minnie should make these and sell them along with her quilts. The work on this is gorgeous. I want one for myself. I love items like these.'

'Minnie makes lots of wee things like this. And Judy stitched the quilted table runners for the shop. The bee ladies sew loads of items including quilted tea cosies.'

Abby tried not to make advertising her default setting, but it was difficult not to think about how to market items like these.

Gordon grinned at her. 'You're trying not to think about how to advertise and sell these, aren't you?'

'No,' she lied. And then she laughed.

Gordon laughed too.

'Okay, so my mind is whirring with ad ideas,' she admitted. 'I can't help it. Give me a few days and all I'll be thinking about is baking cakes and sewing.'

'Speaking of cakes...could you also bake chocolate cakes for me. Ones with a real, rich chocolate flavour and sandwiched with chocolate buttercream would be ideal. Any others you can suggest as well.'

'I'll do that. I can make chocolate fudge cake for you too.'

'Perfect.'

With the cake order agreed, Abby picked up her quilt bag and the box of sweets and headed out.

Gordon walked her to the door. 'I'm quite excited about upgrading my website, and knowing I won't have to bake some of the cakes for the customers lets me push on with my sweet making plans.' He smiled at her. 'Thanks, Abby. I'm glad you've moved here.'

'So am I. I'll deliver some of the cakes tomorrow.'

'See you then,' he said happily. He was so engrossed in thoughts about his website that he didn't tell her he hoped she would have dinner with him.

She smiled at him, stepped outside the shop and felt the sea air sweep through her hair. The breeze had increased and she saw the waves on the water, as if the weather had changed and a storm was brewing.

She walked briskly along the shore, unconcerned about the possibility of a stormy night, because she loved the exhilarating sense of freedom being out in the elements, far away from the city. This is what she'd imagined life would be like here, living in a cosy cottage by the sea. The weather in Scotland had a mind of its own, but she'd always loved rainy days when she could sit by the fire and watch the rain batter off the windows, or shelter under an umbrella and go for a refreshing walk if she was dressed for the downpour. She loved the snow too, and frosty nights when everything sparkled and the air was crisp and fresh. And autumn days when the world glowed with burnished tones of bronze and copper, falling into smoky November nights that reminded her of her past. Although her parents were long gone, she'd had a happy upbringing, filled with encouragement to sew and bake and enjoy the seasons, something she missed and had never quite found in her life of advertising. But maybe here she'd feel at home again, living a life that was far more suited to the things she loved.

As the wind whipped across the sea, she finally reached the cottage, unlocked the door, stepped inside and closed it against the blustery night. She'd left a lamp on, and it provided a welcoming glow as she got ready for bed. Sorting the bed before going to the quilting bee had been sensible, because tiredness was starting to overtake her excitement at being here, and making new friends.

Snuggling under the covers, she pulled the top quilt up and gazed out the window at the sea. The walls of the cottage were thick and the doors and windows were solid barriers against the noise of the approaching storm. It made her feel snug and warm, protected somehow against the onslaught of the world. So she was surprised to see a lone figure run along the shore, a man, wearing a hooded top.

41

Her heart squeezed when she recognised him — Josh! There he was running like a man who refused to be tamed by the elements.

He glanced over at her cottage before running on. He had, hadn't he? She could've been mistaken, and yet in her heart she sensed him look over, a brief connection. There was something about Josh that seemed to disturb her plans for a quaint life baking and quilting in the cottage. She wasn't sure what it was and whether she would suppress her feelings or encourage her heart to be open to new possibilities...

As the wind gathered pace and the storm grew wild outside, she snuggled further under the quilt and went to sleep.

Josh ran against the storm. He'd seen the lights go out in Abby's cottage from a distance and then sprinted on along the shore. He felt unsettled, unsure, two things he hadn't experienced in a long time.

Regrets weren't part of his character. Turning his back on the fight ring was a decision he'd made alone. Even though his father had urged him to hang up his gloves and forgo the chance of a career as a boxer or competitive martial artist, the decision had been his, and he hadn't regretted it. The training was what he loved most, not the fight, simply the challenge against himself to keep fighting fit, strong and capable, attributes that were surely of benefit to him as a young businessman in a world where tenacity and energy were required on a regular basis.

Spits of rain hit off his face as he looked up at the stormy night sky. It would pour soon, so he headed back, running up the narrow path that twisted and wound its way from the shore into the greenery of the fields and trees. The scent of the foliage was intense, and the deeper he ventured, the steeper the climb, causing him to use every muscle in his long–legged thighs to put a spurt on to beat the worst of the rainstorm.

By the time he reached the top his heart was pounding, perhaps not entirely from the exertion. His thoughts were still edged with images of Abby and the way she'd smiled at him earlier, open and honest...and quite beautiful.

He pushed back the hood of his top and swept the drops of rain from his troubled brow as he ran the last few steps, trying to brush away such thoughts of her, especially as he had to deal with her on a business basis the following afternoon. Whatever had urged him to invite her to tea he'd never know. The invitation was out of his mouth before he'd had time to consider the consequences. And what if she took him up on his offer to bring her quilts for a photo–shoot? What a mess he'd gotten himself into. He liked Abby. There was something about her that made him want to protect her while knowing she was quite capable of taking care of herself. That conflict of emotions hadn't sat steadily on his broad shoulders.

When her solicitor sent him details of Abby and her acceptance of the cottage, he'd done what his firm always did — checked her background to ensure she really was Netta's relative. From the brief investigation, he'd seen pictures of her, recent photos of her attending functions organised by the advertising agency she worked for. He'd liked her the moment he saw those first photographs and the way she stood out from those around her, as if she was there but wished she was somewhere else. He hoped that somewhere else would be here by the seaside, and that maybe...maybe she'd be as nice as she appeared to be. The glowing comments from her solicitor that she was easy to deal with, very smart and pleasant, certainly appealed to Josh.

He pushed thoughts of Abby aside. He'd never been beaten in the ring, found success as a businessman, so there had to be a part of his life where he was a failure — and that was in the romance arena. The few romances he'd had never worked out.

Sighing wearily, he forged on the last few strides as the bullets of water came sheeting down.

The well worn path led to his house, a mansion, shielded from prying eyes by trees and shrubbery, and yet offering a spectacular view of the sea to those who stood on the balcony that stretched along the second floor of the two–storey structure.

Hurrying inside, he shook the rain from his hair and tore his damp top off.

The house was well–lit but silent. No one was there to welcome him home. It rarely crossed his mind, yet at times like this the cold silence hammered home that he lived alone.

He ran upstairs, stripped off, dried himself, threw on a pair of boxer shorts and thought about getting some sleep. Glass doors opened out from his bedroom on to the balcony. He opened them and gazed outside, enjoying the energy of the storm while being sheltered from the rain.

Far below near the shore he saw Abby's whitewashed cottage standing strong, facing the brunt of the storm blowing in from the sea.

She'd be asleep in bed by now, he thought. Something he should do.

Abby was awake so early the daylight hadn't yet gathered the strength to penetrate the grey mist covering everything outside her bedroom window.

A mild panic hit her and she clutched at the quilt for a second, before realising she was in the cottage and not in her flat in Glasgow. The panic dropped in an instant, but now she was wide awake.

Rather than lie there and churn over all the things she had to do, including baking chocolate cakes par excellence, she got up, washed, dressed in clean clothes and set about her tasks.

First on her agenda was the cake baking. She checked the recipe books, understood what she needed, fired up the ovens while she measured out the ingredients and then started baking the chocolate cakes.

According to the recipe notes, extra cocoa powder was the key ingredient that gave the cakes a real, rich chocolate flavour. These were going to be enticing looking cakes that lived up to expectations and were full of flavour. The second chocolate cake recipe included plenty of cocoa too, was also sandwiched with chocolate buttercream, but coated in milk chocolate instead of dark chocolate frosting.

Abby stared at the mixtures as she whipped up the ingredients. If these cakes tasted half as delicious as she anticipated, she was on to a couple of winners.

The morning started to brighten slightly, and the heavy grey mist lightened to reveal the garden outside the kitchen window. Everything was washed clean from the rain. She opened the back door and breathed in the fresh air that was potent with the floral scent mixed with the sea.

While the remainder of the cakes were baking and others now cooling, she stepped out and had a look around the garden — and a peek inside the shed. She unravelled the rambling roses that had a grip of the key and unlocked the door. It was clean and dry inside and smelled like a potting shed. Garden tools hung from the edge of a shelf and an old–fashioned ladies bicycle rested against the workbench. It was covered with a blanket and she shook it off and admired the pretty pink bike.

She'd loved her bike when she was a girl, but hadn't gone cycling in years. This bike was vintage but sturdy, built to last, though someone had given it a fresh lick of paint and taken care of it. The tires needed a bit of air and she used the bicycle pump to boost them.

Wheeling it outside she had the urge to jump on and go for a ride along the shore. But sensibility calmed her impulse. There were cakes to bake and finish. But maybe she could use it to deliver the cakes to Gordon's tea shop. The basket was large enough to hold the cakes he'd ordered. His delivery was first on her agenda, followed by items for Minnie's grocery shop.

Yes, she decided firmly. This would be her mode of transport this morning. That's if she could remember how to ride a bike, but then there was that old saying...

She reckoned she hadn't forgotten.

Josh stood on the balcony, striped to the waist, wearing only a pair of training trousers. He breathed in the fresh air, feeling the mild cold breeze brush against his toned torso. Sea mist softened the horizon and cloaked the sound of the water lapping on the shore. It also took the edge off his expectations. His first thoughts when getting out of bed before jumping in the shower were of Abby and the pending afternoon tea and promises he might not be able to keep. Broken promises were never his intention when he'd invited her, but thinking through the various scenarios that had kept him awake half the night, there were several things that could go wrong, and only one that could go right.

Taking a calming breath, he relaxed the muscles in his stomach that had tightened from a six to an eight pack just thinking about his predicament. Pearl and the other women from the quilting bee would know his lone wolf type reputation. Maybe they'd already advised Abby to cancel her afternoon meeting. Maybe she was in her cottage right now, gazing out at the sea and wondering how to tell him she was too busy baking or quilting to pop up and sign the letter.

Again, he had to deliberately relax his torso. Twisting himself into a corkscrew wasn't a regular experience. In fact, he was at the core quite a steady person, mainly calm and sensible. He brushed his hair back from his brow. So why was he standing there like a fool having arguments with himself that hadn't even happened?

His phone rang, jarring him from his thoughts.

He hurried inside, picked up his phone from the bedside table and then went back outside on to the balcony as he took the call.

It was Pearl. His heart sank for a moment thinking she'd drawn the short straw to tell him Abby had cancelled.

'Morning, Josh. It's me. As you know, this is my day off, but as I believe you've got a visitor coming to the house for afternoon tea, I wondered if you'd like me to help organise it.'

His reply was immediate. 'No, no, but thank you, Pearl. I want you to enjoy your day off.'

'I don't mind—'

'It's fine,' he cut–in. 'I can manage to make the tea.' He could. He wasn't useless even though staff took care of the household duties. He didn't have any of them living in the mansion, so when he was on his own, which to be fair wasn't often unless it was during the night, he was quite capable of fending for himself.

'Okay,' she chirped. 'Remember, you'll need the nice tea service and napkins. And Abby will expect cake. The fancy type.'

'Cake.' He suppressed the immediate idea to whisk Abby elsewhere for a proper afternoon tea. 'What type of cake would you suggest?'

'A nice raspberry and cream sponge and a chocolate cake. You can't go wrong with either of those.' Even Josh couldn't get those wrong, though remembering what he'd ordered with all good intentions for the staff party, there was no guarantee. The finger buffet they'd had wasn't quite the elaborate dinner he'd intended. He'd made it up to them with a lavish spread a week later, but...

'I'll buy both types, and anything else that looks presentable.' He surprised himself by how capable he sounded.

Pearl was taken aback by Josh's self–assurance. Maybe he could organise the tea and cake fine. She made the offer to be on cavalry standby if things went awry. 'Phone if you need me.' Her tone said it all.

'Thank you, Pearl. Enjoy your day off.'

After the call he wondered where to buy the cakes. He rarely stepped into Minnie's grocery shop. Did she even sell fancy cakes?

Staff such as Pearl took care of all his shopping. Then he remembered the tea shop. He ran past it regularly. Gordon sold cakes and always started work extra early. Although the tea shop wouldn't yet be open, he'd knock on the door. Gordon would let him in. Yes, he'd run down there and buy the fancy cakes. Training and shopping combined. His day was starting to feel organised and less in jeopardy of being derailed by his own impulsiveness.

Josh finished getting dressed and shrugged an empty rucksack on his back. He ran down to the shore and along to the tea shop. On the way, he glanced over at Abby's cottage, but there was no sign of her. He imagined she'd be inside, busy baking cakes.

CHAPTER FIVE

A ladies vintage bicycle leaned against the exterior of the tea shop.

Someone had painted it the palest pink and it had a large basket in front of the handlebars. Josh imagined that Gordon was probably going to fill the basket with flowers. It looked like a prop to enhance the old–fashioned look of the shop.

Josh peered through the windows. The lights shone from the kitchen, so he knew Gordon was in. He knocked on the door.

Moments later, Gordon came hurrying through, wiping the flour from his hands on his apron.

He frowned at Josh through the glass door, unlocked it quickly, thinking something was wrong.

'It's okay, nothing's wrong,' Josh assured him, stepping inside.

Gordon remained perturbed.

Before he could say anything, Josh explained, 'I wanted to buy—' he stopped the second he saw Abby wandering through from the kitchen. She was wearing an apron that matched Gordon's and the same questioning expression.

'To buy what?' Gordon encouraged Josh to continue.

Josh was frozen for a moment.

Gordon smiled at him. 'Is there something up?' Josh had never set foot inside the tea shop since Gordon opened it. He couldn't begin to imagine what had brought him here. They only knew each other from the shore when Gordon went swimming and Josh ran past. Nodding acquaintances.

Abby smiled too, but everything happened in a few moments of condensed curiosity. She didn't get a chance to comment before Josh told them what he wanted.

'I'd like to buy...' Josh eyed the cake display but didn't want Abby seeing what cakes were likely to make it to their afternoon tea. That also ruled out buying scones or anything that hinted he was shopping for their meeting. Although she probably wouldn't have minded, he did. It didn't feel right to be buying the cakes he planned to serve up later.

Gordon gave him time to think, because clearly Josh was in a tizzy.

Josh finally decided what to order, sort of. 'I'd like something for my breakfast.'

Gordon couldn't disguise his surprise. Josh was here buying cakes for breakfast? Noooo. Josh was telling fibs, but seeing the knowing look from one man to another, Gordon went along with the ruse. Sometimes guys had to help each other out.

'I've got fresh baked pancakes.' Gordon motioned to the golden pancakes on display.

'I'll have one of those,' Josh agreed. Anything to get out of the shop.

Gordon frowned. 'Just one?' He popped it in a bag as he spoke.

Josh adjusted his order. 'Two.'

'The potato scones are tasty for breakfast,' Abby suggested.

'I'll have one of those,' said Josh.

Abby gazed at him, wondering what was wrong with him. He looked so tense.

'Two,' Josh added. 'Two potato scones.'

Gordon dropped these carefully into the paper bag and handed the order to Josh.

Josh gave him more money than was needed, and rather than wait for change, he nodded his thanks and hurried out.

Gordon and Abby frowned at each other and then smiled.

'What was that all about?' she said.

'There goes a man way out of his depths,' Gordon said knowingly. 'Whatever Josh is up to, things aren't going as he planned.'

Josh ran faster than he had in some time, spurred on by the need to get as far away from the tea shop as possible. He didn't stop running until he reached the path leading up to his house, and even then he sprinted up it like a man eager to get home where he could rethink his plans in private.

The quietude of the house provided a much needed retreat.

He went up to his bedroom, stood on the balcony and gazed out at the sea. The mist had almost cleared and shards of sunlight shone across the landscape, a sure sign that the day was going to be warm later on. Afternoon tea outside on the patio was a possibility if the weather held steady. Then again, if he set it up in his study, he could present an air of businesslike hospitality while offering Abby tea and cake. That's if he managed to gets his hands on the appropriate cakes. He shook his head and sighed heavily. He wasn't very good at this. He wasn't very good at all when it came to dealing with his feelings for Abby. Give him a business matter and he'd tear through it efficiently. But ask him to organise a pleasant afternoon enjoying tea and cake with a woman that made his heart ache just looking at her...and his good intentions started to unravel faster than he could handle them.

He sighed again, and looked out at the calming sea, and that's when he saw the figure on the pink bicycle riding along the shore road heading for her cottage.

Taking advantage of the situation that Abby wasn't anywhere near the tea shop, he picked up his car keys, ran downstairs, jumped in his sleek black car and drove down to Gordon's shop.

Josh parked outside the tea shop and hurried in. Gordon wasn't open yet for business, but he hadn't locked the door after Abby had left, so Josh was able to go in and ask Gordon to help him out.

Gordon was surprised to see him. Two visits from Josh in one day. But he kept his smart mouth comments to himself. It was obvious that Josh was wound up.

'You probably know that I've asked Abby to have afternoon tea with me today at my house,' Josh began.

'Every detail.'

Instead of being annoyed that his private business was common knowledge, Josh was relieved that he didn't have to explain anything.

'Okay,' said Josh. 'So I need cakes. Fancy cakes. Pearl advised me to buy chocolate cake and some sort of sponge. What would you suggest?'

Gordon went over to a display cabinet and lifted out a classic chocolate cake, sandwiched with buttercream and topped with a smooth layer of chocolate icing. He held it up. 'Pearl's suggestion is ideal.' He put the cake down on the counter without waiting for Josh's approval. It was clear Josh was out of his depth so Gordon made the decisions for him and picked up a lemon drizzle cake.

Josh started to breathe easier, seeing Gordon select the cakes. He looked around, impressed. 'It's a nice place you've got here.'

Gordon put the cakes in boxes. 'Thanks. You might think of dropping in sometimes instead of running by it.' His words weren't meant to sound snippy.

50

Josh didn't take offence. Gordon was right.

'I know you're a busy businessman, Josh, however, there's a whole community down here that you're missing out on. Keeping to yourself up there in your mansion isn't good for you. You need to mix with folks sometimes, have a wee bit of fun. Life isn't all about business.'

Josh nodded. 'I suppose that's how people see me — unapproachable and aloof.'

Gordon put the cake boxes down and issued a few home truths. 'It's worse than that. You've acquired such a reputation for keeping yourself to yourself that they don't even consider you anymore. You're all but invisible. If it wasn't for seeing you run along the shore, nobody would know you even existed.' Gordon lifted the boxes and put them in a bag. 'That's no way for a man like you to live.'

Josh's expression showed that Gordon's comments had cut through him.

'I'm not getting at you,' Gordon emphasised. 'I'm just—'

'No, you're right. I need to...' he wasn't sure what he needed to do first.

'Buy these cakes and make a half decent effort to present a pleasant afternoon tea for Abby,' Gordon told him.

Josh agreed and paid for the cakes. 'Was Abby working with you this morning?'

'No, she dropped the cakes off extra early, then she stayed to chat. I was working in the kitchen, and she put an apron on and helped me bake the scones while I cooked the pancakes.'

'Chatting about baking were you?'

'A bit, but mainly talking about my tea shop. She's helping me advertise my confectionery range on my website. I'm gleaning information on advertising the products to full advantage.'

'Ah, yes, her advertising expertise is handy.'

'I'm not taking advantage of her. We're all trying to help each other. Abby's helping the quilting bee ladies set up in business with a new website to sell their quilts.' Gordon explained the details.

Josh listened carefully. 'So she's sparked them into creating an online business?'

'She has. All the ladies are excited. They're planning on taking photos of their quilts here at my tea shop to put on their website.'

'And Abby initiated this from a night at the quilting bee?'

Gordon nodded. 'She's quite generous at sharing her knowledge and very encouraging. The quilting bee was buzzing last night.'

'Are they looking for investors?'

Gordon laughed. 'This is their hobby, Josh, not one of your conglomerates or whatever it is you deal with.'

'No, of course,' Josh said, reining in his automatic response to advise on business matters.

'But it's not up to me to speak for them. You should mention this to them yourself. Tell Abby. See if she thinks they'd benefit from having an investor. I assume you're meaning yourself?'

'Yes.' He smiled. 'It's hard to switch off from business mode.'

'That's exactly why you need to broaden your horizons, look around and see that there's a whole life here, with people you barely know.'

Josh felt as if he'd been flipped inside out. Gordon's comments were something to consider.

Gordon spoke about the cakes. 'Abby baked the chocolate cake, and she said she was tempted to keep it for herself. It's Netta's recipe and Abby hasn't even had a chance to taste a slice, so I know she'll like this, even if it is a bit odd serving her something she baked herself. It'll work, trust me.'

'Okay. What's the other cake?'

'Lemon drizzle. I baked it. Abby had her eye on it this morning and commented that it looked delicious, so it's a win–win situation with these two cakes.'

Josh lifted the bag of cakes from the counter and paid for them. 'I appreciate your help.'

'You're very welcome.'

Josh turned to leave and then hesitated. 'You like Abby, don't you?' He could tell by the way Gordon's voice was filled with warmth and admiration when he spoke about her.

'I do.' Gordon looked straight at him. 'And obviously so do you.'

Josh nodded.

For a moment there was an understanding between two men that they both liked the same woman. There was no sense of bitter rivalry, just an acknowledgment of the situation.

'Thanks again for your help, Gordon.'

'Anytime. Enjoy your cakes.'

Josh left, got into his car and drove off.

Gordon locked the front door, went upstairs and changed into his trunks. The tea shop didn't open until later in the morning, and this allowed him time for his daily dip in the sea.

He ran the short distance on to the sand and quite liked that a thin layer of mist still lingered over the water. He dived in and started swimming along the shoreline, feeling like he was floating between the sea and the clouds. The best feeling in the world. Except perhaps for falling a little bit in love with Abby, something he wasn't going to encourage himself to do, because deep in his heart he sensed that Josh's feelings for her were stronger than his. Or perhaps he was wrong. Only time would tell.

Abby weighed the eggs in their shells and calculated the exact ratio of flour, sugar and cocoa powder needed for the next order of cakes. These were for Minnie. The recipe was precise and required adjusting according to the size of eggs that were used for the cake mix.

While these were baking, she tackled the first batch of shortbread, feeling more confident about that due to her recent training. The recipe was similar to the one she'd used before with only a few tweaks to make it extra special.

Although she tried to concentrate on the baking, she kept thinking about Josh and his behaviour earlier at the tea shop. Those grey eyes of his had looked so surprised to see her there with Gordon. He'd probably explain everything later when she went to his house.

Her heart quickened every time she thought about their meeting. She wondered what quilts to take with her. Two of her favourites probably — the quilt with butterfly appliqué and the floral one she'd sewn recently with all the pretty remnants of fabric from her stash.

She pictured what Josh's house would look like. The word mansion made her think of a sweeping staircase, large rooms with ornate furnishing and luxurious rugs on the floors. From the glimpse of it lit up the previous night, it had numerous rooms and a balcony that she presumed gave a great view of the sea. Maybe Josh could see her cottage from there.

The cottage suited her, and she supposed the mansion suited Josh. Her world was cosy and she enjoyed the small comforts of home. Being alone in a mansion didn't particularly appeal to her, but from everything the ladies had said about Josh, he seemed to like it. Maybe sharing it with someone would be different. Not that she thought she'd ever live there with Josh.

She felt herself blush just thinking about him. She'd surely blush being there with him, signing the letter. She hadn't blushed so much since her teens, and hadn't anticipated meeting such a handsome looking man here.

Pearl had confirmed that Josh was a fighter, but skimped on the details. Minnie had whispered later during the quilting bee that he'd given up a career in boxing and martial arts to concentrate on his business.

'Is that why he still runs and looks fighting fit?' Abby had whispered to Minnie.

'Yes. Pearl doesn't think he regrets giving up the fighting. He enjoys his work. He's smart and makes a lot of money from it, and from investing in other companies. That's the reason he's away a lot of the time, due to his stock market work.'

'What about his family?' Abby had asked in a hushed tone.

'There's only his father left.' Minnie had glanced to see that Pearl didn't overhear her telling Abby Josh's secrets. 'They were never close. Josh lives his own life. He's successful financially, but a lone wolf. And he hasn't had a steady girlfriend that he's happy with according to the gossip.'

One of the ovens pinged, nudging Abby from her thoughts of Josh. She put on her oven gloves, took the cakes out and put them on a cooling rack.

From the kitchen window she could see the field adjoining her garden and the countryside leading up to the hills where Josh lived. Would she at least be friends with him? She felt an easy friendship towards Gordon already. Or would her meeting be the only time she'd be in Josh's mansion? All her instincts told her there was something about Josh that promised more from their afternoon meeting. That was why she was glad to be busy baking, making the time go in. She felt excited and nervous in equal measures.

Her phone rang, startling her from her deep thoughts.

It was Minnie.

'Just a quick call,' Minnie said, sounding furtive. 'Josh is in a tizzy about his afternoon tea meeting with you. Gordon popped in and told me what happened at the tea shop.'

'Josh bought pancakes and potato scones that he really didn't seem to want,' Abby added.

'You're right, because after you left, he drove down and bought cakes from Gordon. And apparently Gordon told him a few home truths about his standoffish behaviour.'

'Was there an argument?'

'No, no, nothing like that. It was all very amiable, just Gordon advising him to be more sociable here. Good advice.' She paused. 'Oh and Josh bought one of the chocolate cakes you baked and a lemon drizzle, so remember to look surprised.'

'He's bought my chocolate cake?'

Voices sounded in the background of the grocery shop.

'Sorry, I have to go,' said Minnie. 'The shop is getting busy. We'll chat later. Enjoy your romantic rendezvous with Josh.'

'Romantic what?' Abby gasped, but Minnie had gone, leaving Abby to feel more nervous than ever.

She hurried to prepare Minnie's cake order so she could go along and find out more details of what was going on. The buttercream was whipped up in jig time, and she put on a spurt of efficiency when it came to decorating them with a melted milk chocolate topping and rich frosting. Instead of overthinking and fussing with them, they turned out smooth and looking rather nice.

Euan was in his field when he saw Abby jump on her bicycle and race off down the shore road. Her basket was loaded with stuff, cakes probably. He'd heard she'd been busy baking since she arrived, and she certainly looked like she was in a hurry as she peddled away with her legs moving like pistons and the wind blowing through her hair. She may not like or trust him, however he couldn't help but admire her spirit. Not many city girls he knew would've thrown themselves so wholeheartedly and quickly into the community. He had to remind himself that Abby was an outsider. Somehow she'd become part of the hub of things without him having had a proper chance to apologise.

Abby parked her bike outside the grocery shop, grabbed half of the cake delivery and hurried inside. Bracken was snuggled in his basket and too comfy to jump up, but his tail wagged when he saw Abby.

Minnie was serving a customer, so Abby put the order down on the counter and went out to bring in the rest of the delivery.

The customer left as she put everything down in front of Minnie.

Abby was slightly out of breath from hurrying. 'What were you saying about romance with Josh?'

Minnie smiled. 'Is that what all the rush is for?'

Abby smiled back at her. 'Yes, you can't say something like that and not expect me to wonder what's being talked about.'

'Well,' Minnie began, 'Gordon and Josh had a bit of a man to man chat, and Josh revealed that he likes you.'

Abby's heart lurched. 'Josh likes me?'

Minnie winked. 'You know what I mean. He *likes* you.'

'Are you sure?'

'Oh, yes. The cake buying fiasco says it all. Josh is determined to impress you.'

'He told Gordon all this?'

'More or less. They both admitted they like you. It was a cards on the table chat.'

Abby stared at Minnie.

'So you've got two handsome admirers.'

'You told me there's always interest when a newcomer arrives,' Abby reasoned. 'I can't take them seriously.'

'I think you should, especially Josh.' Minnie lowered her tone. 'Come on, surely you like him.'

Abby blushed.

Minnie took this as her answer. 'Well then, you should be thinking about what to wear this afternoon and not fussing over other things.'

'I didn't expect to be thinking about romance until I was settled in the cottage for a while.'

'Listen, it's just tea and cake with Josh. Go up there with good intentions and see if you both get along. You'll know in yourself whether there's a real spark between you.'

Abby breathed deeply. 'You're right. I'll enjoy having tea and tasting the cake I baked.'

Minnie acknowledged the order Abby had made for her. 'Thanks for the cakes. I'll settle up the money with you shortly. First, what are you planning to wear this afternoon? A nice wee dress I presume?'

Abby looked blank.

'You do have a dress with you?' Minnie asked her.

'Yes, I have a little black dress that—'

Minnie cut–in. 'No. Nothing too formal. What else have you got?'

Abby mentally ran through the dresses she had. 'Only a few, and they're more like cocktail and evening dresses. I wore them to social functions organised by the ad agency.'

'What about a tea dress or something like that?' Minnie asked.

'No, so maybe I could wear trousers and a top.'

'That'll not do. What you need is a lovely wee dress.' Minnie picked up her phone and made a call. 'Judy, we've got a dress emergency. Abby has nothing nice to wear for her tryst with Josh.' She paused. 'Okay, thanks, I'll send her round right now.' She finished the call. 'Pop along to Judy's bar restaurant. They've got a house further up the hillside, but also stay above the premises. Judy's got lots of dresses and will sort you out.'

'I don't want to be any bother.'

Minnie brushed Abby's reluctance aside. 'On you go. Judy's wardrobe is bursting with clothes. She buys loads and sews some herself. She's got a neat figure and is bound to have something to fit you. Trust me, she's happy to help.'

'Okay,' Abby agreed.

Minnie waved her off. 'See you later.'

Abby wheeled her bicycle along to the bar restaurant and was welcomed in by Judy.

'I've got a couple of dresses in mind.' Judy sounded enthusiastic as she whisked Abby through the bar and led her upstairs.

The bar restaurant had a mellow atmosphere and was a lot more stylish than Abby had imagined. The whole place was quiet and wasn't open for business until later in the day. Judy's husband, Jock, was behind the bar, stocking the shelves with wine and spirits, and gave her a wave as she went past. Abby smiled over at him. He looked fit and strong and had a cheery grin.

Part of the bar was a restaurant area, and there was an extension that was used for parties and functions. A poster advertising ceilidh dancing was pinned up, and another one listed things that were happening on various nights throughout the week. Everything from the polished bar area with a wonderful selection of whisky, to the deep burgundy carpeting and table settings showed that Judy and Jock took care to make every aspect look inviting.

Judy spoke to Abby as they went upstairs. 'I'm glad you're here because I wanted to ask you something about the quilting bee website.'

Abby followed her into the bedroom where two wardrobes full of Judy's clothes were open to view. Minnie hadn't been exaggerating when she said Judy had plenty of dresses.

'What did you want to ask me?' said Abby, watching Judy flick through the clothes hanging up and selecting several dresses.

'Would it be okay if I used a similar template for the bee website that we use for the bar restaurant? It's a handy layout and easy to update. We could choose a theme and customise the design to suit the quilting bee, but this would make it simple to get it up and running.'

'That's a sensible idea, Judy.'

Judy was pleased. 'Great, I'll make a start on it, and then we can all agree on the type of theme we want.' She then picked up one of the dresses. The fabric had a pretty floral print. 'Okay, let's get you a dress. What do you think of this one?' Judy held it up. 'A classic tea dress, a wrap over, so you can adjust the waist to fit.'

Abby liked it immediately. 'It's lovely.'

Judy was sure she'd picked the right one. 'Try it on.'

Abby put it on and looked at herself in the full length mirror. 'I love it.' The length was ideal and the short sleeves and neat waistline was very flattering.

'I've only worn it once.'

Abby smoothed her hands over the soft jersey. 'The fabric is gorgeous.'

'I picked it myself.'

Abby paused. 'Did you make this dress?'

'Yes, I love dressmaking, which is just as well as I love dresses. I buy them too, but I enjoy sewing. I used to work as a dressmaker before I got married.'

'This is beautiful work, Judy.'

Judy beamed and held up another dress. 'Try this one on too. It's a similar design but different fabric. A ditsy daisy print. Quite pretty.'

Abby tried the second dress on.

'That suits you too, though I think the first one is the winner for your meeting with Josh. Very classy. Perfect for afternoon tea.'

'I really appreciate you letting me borrow a dress,' said Abby.

'Do you have shoes and a bag to go with it?'

'Yes.'

Judy smiled happily and popped the two dresses in a bag while Abby changed back into her own clothes. 'Here you are.'

'I'll take good care of them,' Abby promised.

'You keep them. I've got plenty.'

Abby went to object, but Judy wouldn't hear of it.

Kitted out with the dresses, Abby popped in to show Minnie what Judy had given her, and then cycled back to the cottage.

CHAPTER SIX

Abby followed Minnie's directions as she drove to Josh's house. Minnie had scribbled a rough map on a paper bag from the grocery shop showing her how to get there. It was a twisted route along the narrow country road and through the trees, and seemed to double back on itself at one point, but Minnie had assured her this was the easiest way to drive up to the secluded mansion from the shore.

A patchwork of fields, farms, cottages and countryside was stitched together by a narrow road threading its way through the fabric of the landscape, piecing everything together along the length of the bay from the sea to the hilltops. The road was barely visible from the shore. Disguised by the trees, it sank seamlessly into the grassland without disturbing the scenery.

Abby had set off early in her car to allow time to navigate the meandering route. Minnie's makeshift map sat on the passenger seat where Abby could glance at it at each point of the journey. Minnie had marked specific things to look out for — a bluebell niche encircling a chestnut tree, a banking of yellow gorse, a bronze lantern beside a farmer's gate, and an old beehive painted pastel blue that had been part of the route for years. Abby saw them all, and mentally ticked them off like items on a treasure trail.

The warm afternoon sun shone through the open window and flickered through the branches of the trees that arched high above the road. The scent of the countryside and the sea reminded her of holidays she'd dreamed of but never had during her busy last few years in the city.

The easy pace of the drive allowed her to view several cottages tucked into hidden niches, and she realised these were some of the properties she'd seen whose windows were aglow in the evening.

Along the way were flowers growing wild that no one wanted to tame — bluebells, daisies, marigolds and roses, reminiscent of the flowers in the fabric of her dress.

Abby wore the floral tea dress Judy had given her. She'd accessorised it with court shoes in a neutral tone and opted for a large shoulder bag containing more items than she possibly required. Nervousness had made her pack several things as back–up, including her laptop and a mini sewing kit. Although it was a long shot she'd need to sew anything, she'd packed it anyway. She also had another bag containing four quilts, doubling her original plan of two favourites. So if she had to show Josh her sewing skills, such as top stitching a quilt, she was armed and ready.

The extra two quilts were chosen to show him one of her modern quilts and to give examples of her range. One depicted a night sky, in midnight blues with stars at the top of the design that faded in a gradation of sapphire and cobalt tones to a row of different coloured little houses. Each house was pieced and stitched using a mix of solids and prints. Every roof, door and window had its own curiosity, created entirely from cotton fabric and quilted with cotton thread. The roofs were solid colours, stripes or polka dots. Ditsy prints were used for the doors and windows. Every part of the design was neatly stitched.

Seahorses and shells were included in the other quilt's appliqué. It had a sea theme in turquoise and aquamarine solids and prints that she hoped Josh would appreciate. This one had taken her longer to make than the night sky with houses, due to the detailed quilting on the seahorses and the sea glass effect. She'd sewn it months ago before she even knew she'd be living in a cottage beside the sea. It had been folded away since the day she'd finished it, and she only remembered it when searching through her quilts to find something less flowery that Josh might prefer.

In her bag she'd also popped some fat quarter pieces of fabric from her stash — a Scottish thistle print, heather, bee and butterfly printed cotton, to show him how she made her quilts from scratch.

The road swept deeper into the landscape as she continued to drive along, wondering if her visit with him would be short and sweet or last the entire afternoon.

She caught her first glimpse of his two–storey mansion through the trees, and followed the narrow route that opened out into a lovely expanse of well–cared for gardens surrounding Josh's property. The whole house looked like money.

His sleek dark car was the only vehicle in the driveway, and she parked beside it.

A quick glance in the mirror showed the trepidation in her eyes. No amount of carefully applied mascara could disguise the excited but anxious look in her wide blue eyes.

Realising he could be watching her, she glanced away, not wanting him to think she was checking her hair and makeup. She'd worn her hair down and added a deep rose lipstick instead of her normal natural makeup tones. It suited the look she had wearing the tea dress. No blusher though. The one thing she didn't need.

Josh appeared at the front door of the mansion as she stepped out of her car. His heart pounded like mad when he saw her, though he tried to hide his reaction behind a casual, welcoming smile. But oh my, he hadn't been prepared for her to look so beautiful, wearing a classic dress and smiling back at him.

'I hope you didn't have any trouble finding the house,' he began, thinking he sounded nervous. 'It's a bit of a twisty–turny road.'

'No.' She reached into the car and showed him the paper bag. 'Minnie drew me a map.'

'Good on Minnie.' He tried not to smile too much as he wasn't sure whether he should or not. He never expected she'd have a map to his house drawn on a grocery shop bag.

'I brought some of my quilts with me.' She shrugged her voluminous bag on to her shoulder, opened the boot of her car and lifted out the large bag containing the four quilts.

Josh strode over. His clothes were businesslike — tailored dark trousers, white shirt and grey silk tie. Like his house, he looked like money.

'Let me get those for you,' he insisted.

In the sunlight his dark hair was silky smooth, brushed back from his handsome features, and her heart squeezed in anticipation of spending the afternoon with this gorgeous man.

He carried the quilts and led her towards the mansion.

'You've got a beautiful house,' she said, 'and the garden looks lovely.'

'I'm glad you like it. I'll show you around the garden later. I thought we'd get our business dealt with first and then have tea.'

She stepped into the mansion's hallway and paused. The interior lived up to her expectations, including the sweeping staircase. Add a reception desk and it could double as a plush hotel. The styling was classy rather than fussy, and apart from their chatter, the house was silent.

He sensed her wondering why it was so quiet. 'It's just the two of us this afternoon. I have regular staff. I couldn't run a place this size on my own and attend to business. However, I like to have days when the staff are off and I've got it all to myself.' He realised he sounded like the lone wolf type Gordon had warned him to avoid.

'I'd do the same,' she said before he could amend his comment. She gazed around. 'I'd want it to feel like my own home.'

Relieved that she agreed with his method of running the place, he put the quilts down on the hall table and led her through to his study. She thought it looked like the type of study a man like Josh would have. A large desk, expensive computer, the latest in design, blended with an antique dresser along one wall that also housed a filing cabinet from an equally classy bygone era. It had plush carpeting, light cream decor and large glass doors that opened out on to a patio and manicured lawn beyond.

He motioned to the letter on his desk. 'I wrote the letter last night. It's straightforward and not really necessary, but handy if I'm not around to protect you and someone questions your right to sell quilts from the cottage.'

She heard every word, but one stood out loud and clear — *protect*. Josh thought to protect her. And he liked her. What if Minnie and Judy were right in their assumptions of a romance brewing...?

'Take your time reading it,' he said, thinking her hesitation was due to the contents of the letter instead of the heart–pounding thoughts of romance with him.

She read the letter, and the wording was clear. Perfect in fact. 'I'm happy to sign it.' She glanced around the desk, wondering which one of the expensive pens she should use.

Josh lifted the nearest pen and handed it to her. For a second their eyes met, closer than she'd ever gazed into those gorgeous grey eyes of his. The feelings he stirred in her made her almost drop the pen.

He pointed to the letter. 'Sign and date it there, then I'll add my signature.'

She did as he asked, then repeated the process with a copy for him. He filed his away in the cabinet.

He folded her letter and popped it in a white envelope. 'Keep this somewhere safe.'

Abby put it her bag.

Josh rubbed his hands together, pleased that the business part of their meeting was done with. 'I thought with it being a sunny afternoon, we could have tea outside.'

'That would be lovely. It's such a nice day.' She assumed he'd lead her out on to the patio from his study and was surprised when he led her into the main hallway to the sweeping staircase. The banister begged to have her slide down it, even just once. She'd loved misbehaving in a fun sort of way when she was a little girl.

He lifted the quilts from the hall table as he walked past and carried them with him.

'There's a great view of the sea from the front lounge balcony,' he said, striding up the stairs.

Abby followed him. So far, everything from the staircase to plush carpeting and expensive decor matched her expectations.

The lounge was also as stylish as she'd imagined, and light and airy. He put the quilts down on a table and led her out on to the balcony.

The view was magnificent, offering a panoramic look along the bay. The shore road was in clear view, as was her cottage that looked small but sweet between the countryside and the sea.

He leaned on the balcony and surveyed the scene. He pointed to her cottage. 'There's your property,' he said, acknowledging he could see it, but had no choice as it was part of the view. The balcony overlooked the scenery, and although he could see where she stayed, the trees hid his mansion from those peering up from the shore. In the evenings, the lights from the mansion could be seen, but it was still well disguised.

'It's quite a distance for you to run each day,' she commented. 'I guess it keeps you fit.' He certainly looked fit, standing there so near that she could detect the fresh scent of his aftershave. Josh smelled as gorgeous as he looked.

'There's a pathway I use that leads directly down to the shore. It's a quicker route if you ever want to run up here rather than drive.'

Abby laughed. 'I'm not quite in your league of fitness. But swimming and cycling should start to get me in better shape.'

He wanted to comment that he thought she was in great shape, but buttoned his lips, though it didn't prevent him from admiring her neat figure in the dress she was wearing.

64

'I heard that you were a boxer or some sort of fighter.' She hoped to encourage him to tell her about this part of his life.

He made light of his fighting ability. 'It's something I did in the past. I gave it up to concentrate on business. I haven't been in the ring for a while. Now I train only for myself.'

He steered the conversation away from his fitness and brought it back to their afternoon tea.

There was a table set with a white linen cover and a small vase of flowers in the middle.

Josh gazed up at the sky. The sun was warm and there was barely a cloud. 'I thought we could have our tea on the balcony.'

Abby nodded, thinking how perfect this would be.

'I'll pop downstairs and get things organised.' He glanced at the tea trolley in the lounge that was already laden with the best tea service, as Pearl had advised him, and the two cakes he'd bought. There was also a tin of luxury shortbread and chocolates.

'Would you like me to give you hand?' she offered.

'No, it's fine. You relax. I'll get the kettle on for the tea. Is tea okay? I have coffee if you prefer.'

'Tea for me.'

Smiling, though slightly less confident than a moment ago, Josh headed downstairs to prepare the tea.

Abby sensed he was nervous, maybe as on edge as she was, so instead of standing admiring the view, she made herself useful and set up the teacups, saucers, side plates and cutlery on the table. She wasn't sure whether to slice the cakes, but decided it was better to leave them on the trolley in the lounge. She'd offer when he came up with the tea, which was remarkably soon.

'Here we are,' he said, carrying two large tea pots of tea and one filled with hot water on a tray. He looked relieved that she'd set the table.

'Oh, great. Thanks, Abby.' He put the tea down and then wasn't sure what he should do next.

Abby jumped in and offered to cut the cakes.

'Do you want me to cut these while you pour the tea?' She stood in the lounge and motioned to the cakes on the tea trolley.

He welcomed her assistance. 'Yes.'

'Chocolate cake or lemon drizzle?' she said, holding the knife poised ready.

'Why don't we have both? I'd like the chocolate first. I believe you baked it and it looks delicious.'

Abby smiled anxiously. Hopefully it would taste as good as it looked.

She pressed the knife carefully through the layer of milk chocolate topping and cut two wedges of the cake. Then she used a clean knife to slice the lemon drizzle cake. The aromatic aroma of the chocolate mixed with the lemon, and even though she was nervous her appetite stirred ready to enjoy tasting the chocolate cake she'd baked.

She placed the slices down on plates and put them on the silver cake stand. Then she lifted the stand outside.

They sat down opposite each other. Josh poured the tea and they helped themselves to slices of chocolate cake.

Thankfully, the cake lived up to Abby's expectations, and she enjoyed the smooth milk chocolate coating with the full flavour of the sponge and buttercream.

Josh kept nodding as he ate it. 'This is what a chocolate cake should taste like.'

'Netta's recipe is great,' said Abby.

'As is the way you've baked it,' he added.

He smiled at her, causing her heart to flutter nervously. Here she was, sitting on the balcony in the warm afternoon sunlight with the man she'd been dealing with via her solicitor for weeks. If only she'd known what he looked like and that she'd be his guest here, just the two of them, sipping tea and eating the cake she'd baked in a cottage she'd barely had a chance to call home.

'Do you do this often? Sit out here?' she asked him. For in her mind she knew that she would. If she lived in a mansion like this, she'd sit outside on the balcony, breathing in the sea air and sew her quilts.

'Not often enough, especially recently, because I've been very busy with work. I've been away a lot, not quite settled, though I plan to change my routine, beginning with enjoying this afternoon here with you.'

She wasn't sure how to react. Outwardly she smiled pleasantly. He'd mentioned business, being busy with work, reasonable enough comments, and yet inwardly she sensed he was telling her that he planned to settle down. Concerned that she was reading too much into things, she sipped her tea and tried not the blush at his compliment.

'Fortunately, all the main rooms on the upstairs floor have access to the balcony,' he continued. 'My two favourite rooms are this lounge and my bedroom.' He motioned behind her.

Abby glanced round and saw that the next room balcony had a sun lounge chair on it. Even the thought of Josh's bedroom sent her blushes into overdrive. Luckily the sea breeze helped to cool her senses, but he noticed her flushed cheeks and realized he'd said something inappropriate.

'I wasn't hinting that my bedroom is next door,' he said. 'I just meant that I relax there when I'm not busy, or after a long day sitting at my desk downstairs in the study. Weather permitting,' he added. His voice had an urgency to redress the balance of things. The last thing he wanted was to give her the impression he'd invited her up to his house for more than tea and chit–chat.

'I'm sure you weren't meaning that. I'm just...' she sighed and decided to be completely honest with him. 'Look where I am. I didn't imagine I'd be here with you when I set off from the city. I've hardly had a chance to unwind since I moved into the cottage. It's great that I've been welcomed by people like the ladies at the quilting bee. I'm even wearing a dress that Judy gave me. It's just a bit overwhelming and...'

His encouraged her to continue. 'And...?'

'And I think I'm afraid to enjoy it too much, to believe it's the fresh start I was hoping for, in case it's simply the excitement of moving here.'

He'd learned to be quite a good judge of character from all the business deals he'd cut with people set on playing games with him. He knew Abby was being straightforward and truthful. His heart twisted, wanting to assure her that he'd do his utmost to make this fresh start as real as he could make it. But past experience and the heartache of romances gone wrong, made him keep his tone calm and not too personal. Although he wanted to put his reassuring arms around her, he sat where he was and spoke plainly.

'You'll settle into the life here soon enough. It's only normal that you have misgivings about things because it's been a whirlwind welcome — starting with Euan's stupid approach to buy the cottage, and then a night at the quilting bee encouraging the ladies to go into business.'

She nodded, agreeing with him.

He smiled gently at her, hoping she'd see the funny side of things.

'Then there's the fiasco I caused at Gordon's tea shop. I'm sure you knew I'd no intention of buying pancakes and potato scones.'

Abby started to smile. 'You looked like you didn't know what to do with them.'

'Seeing you there with Gordon caught me off guard. I thought the pink bike was a prop, not your mode of transport.'

She giggled. 'My thighs are aching from all the manic peddling. It's definitely going to get me fit.'

'That and diving into the sea in the morning — not commando, with your swimwear on,' he teased her.

Abby laughed and hid her face in her hands. 'I was so embarrassed when I said that.'

He leaned forward. 'I'll make a deal with you. Let's not act like a couple of fools around each other.'

Abby smiled at him.

He reached across the table and offered her his hand. 'Deal?'

She shook hands with him. 'Deal.'

For the first time she didn't blush like a schoolgirl, though the touch of Josh's firm handshake did feel good. Although he'd been a fighter, his hands bore no sign of roughness and felt strong, elegant and smooth.

They enjoyed their tea and cake, including the lemon drizzle cake, and chatted about the locale and his stocks and shares business. The fluttering excitement she felt was still there, but they were getting to know each other without awkward blushes and embarrassing comments stirring up trouble.

Josh put his napkin down after they'd finished their tea. He stood up. 'Come on, I'd like to see the quilts you brought with you.'

They went inside to the lounge and Abby lifted the quilts from the bag.

'These are beautiful.' He seemed genuinely interested in her work, and was particularly taken with the sea theme quilt. 'I like them all, but I love the sea, and this captures the feeling of it with these lovely blues. I expected all your quilts to be like this one.' He pointed to the traditional floral one.

'A sew various designs, traditional and modern.'

'Do you want to take some pictures of them?' He glanced out at the sunshine. 'We could photograph them in the garden while the sun's out, and then set them up here in the lounge or elsewhere.'

'Yes, the colours will show up well in the daylight.'

Josh lifted the quilts and they went downstairs and out into a part of the garden that had roses and a hazel tree.

'How tall are you?' she asked him.

He frowned. 'Six–two.'

'Perfect.'

He gave her a wry grin. 'Perfect for what?'

'For holding the quilts up so I can take pictures of them.'

He shook his head, looking embarrassed. 'I don't want to be in the photos, Abby.'

'You won't be.' She showed him how to hold up the first quilt to show the design while he was hidden behind it. 'Your fingers are peeping out at the top edge. Grip it a bit lower so you're completely hidden.'

He did as she asked, quite happy to get involved, so happy that he started laughing as he held the quilt up. The quilt was about six feet by four feet, and the colours of the fabric and butterflies in the design looked great in the sunlight.

'Stand still,' she hissed at him, trying not to laugh at what she'd persuaded him to do.

Josh continued to laugh.

'Hold it steady so I can get a crisp picture of the quilt,' she said, laughing.

'You're laughing too, Abby.'

'You're making me laugh, so stop it,' she scolded playfully.

Josh took a deep breath and held the quilt steady.

Abby snapped pictures with her phone. 'Okay, you can relax. These will work fine for my website.'

Josh folded the quilt and held up the next one without her having to ask him. 'Do you want me to stand facing another direction so you have a different background for the photos?'

This man was too good to be true, she thought. 'Yes, stand over there, so I can capture the flowers.' They went so well with the floral quilt.

They repeated this process with all four quilts, finishing with the night sky one using the background of the mansion.

Abby clicked her phone off and went over to Josh. 'Thanks. Your arms must be aching holding the quilts up.'

Josh sort of nodded. He didn't want to say that his arms and shoulders didn't feel any different from all the effort.

Abby pressed her lips together. Of course his arms wouldn't be sore. He had leanly muscled arms that could send her wild if they were ever wrapped around her. And then she blushed.

For the first time he commented, 'You're blushing.'

'I'm not,' she lied.

'You are.' He grinned at her.

Did he know what she was thinking?

She folded one of the quilts and tried not to blush.

'Will we go inside now and take photos in the lounge?' he suggested.

'Yes,' she said, and let him lead the way upstairs.

The lounge was the ideal setting and Abby draped the quilts on the couches and chairs.

While she checked the pictures on her phone, and then on her laptop, Josh came over and peered at them. 'Oh yes, these look stylish. Do you want me to take any photos of you with the quilts?'

'Me?'

'Customers will want to see pictures of you, and as you're looking lovely in your dress...' he paused and held his hand out.

She gave him her phone. 'Okay. Just a couple.'

Josh snapped more than she needed, and she appreciated his help.

'It's a pity we haven't any shots of you making your quilts, or sewing a piece of fabric.'

Abby dug the sewing kit out of her bag. 'I came prepared.'

'Prepared for what?'

She pulled out the fat quarters of fabric she'd brought with her. And a rotary cutter, quilting templates, thread and a selection of patterns.

70

'What else do you have in the depths of that bag of yours?' Josh laughed. 'I'm half expecting you to pull out a parasol and a folding chair.'

'Very funny, Josh.'

She sat on one of the sofas and pretended to stitch a piece of fabric. Josh took close–up pictures of her working.

Afterwards, he handed the phone to her. 'There you go.'

'Thanks for going along with this, Josh,' she said, packing everything away again in her bag.

'I'm happy to help.' Then he became thoughtful. 'I do have another setting you may want to include, but please don't think I'm being forward by suggesting you put the quilts on my bed. After all, that's where most people use them.'

'Your bedroom?' Even the thought of it. But he was right. 'Okay.'

With Josh leading the way, they went into his bedroom. The colour scheme was cream and pale blue and total luxury from the soft carpeting to the silk sheets. Oh yes, she thought, this man had silk sheets on his bed. She didn't think she'd ever slept in a bed with silk sheets, and certainly not at home. Her sheets were cotton — sensible, soft and cosy. She'd always thought of silk sheets as being...well...sensual.

Unaware of where her thoughts were leading her, Josh had laid the traditional floral quilt on his double bed. The quilt was large enough to suit it.

His bedroom was tidy, clean and fresh, and like the lounge, glass doors opened out on to the balcony. The doors were open and the sea air wafted in, and she imagined what it would be like to lie down on a bed like this and relax on a warm sunny day or hot night.

Josh was staring at her. 'Do you want me to change the quilt?' he asked, thinking her hesitation was due to her not liking what he'd set up.

She blinked and pushed her wayward thoughts aside to concentrate on taking the photos. 'No, it's fine.' She snapped several pictures of it, and then when she went to lift it off the bed, Josh stopped her.

'No, I like that quilt. I'd like to keep it. I'll buy it and the sea theme quilt. I'm assuming they're for sale?'

'Well, yes, but—'

'Use the photos of them on your website. They show your range of designs, but mark them as sold. I'll pay whatever you're asking for them.'

'Are you sure? You really don't have to—'

'I like the quilts, Abby.'

'Okay, and thanks.'

Josh smiled at her. There was no hint of underhandedness in what he'd done. She really did believe he liked the quilts.

She smiled at him as she collected her things ready to leave. 'I've had a nice time.'

'So have I.' He paused. 'Do you have to go? I could make more tea.'

Before she could reply, her phone rang. It was Minnie.

'Hello, Minnie.' She glanced at Josh. He wandered over to the balcony but could still hear the conversation.

'Did you find Josh's mansion okay?' Minnie asked.

'Yes, thanks for the map.'

'Judy and I were wondering if you were all right?'

'I am. I'm here with Josh taking photos of my quilts.'

'So he's there with you?'

'Yes.'

'Can he hear me?' Minnie whispered.

'No.'

'Has he kissed you yet?' Minnie asked loudly.

Abby gasped. 'What?'

'Has Josh made a pass at you?'

'No,' Abby whispered. 'We had a lovely afternoon tea.'

'Oh, right, so you can't explain because he's listening. Tell us all the details later. Judy's invited a few of us to the bar restaurant tonight at seven so we can talk about the quilting bee website. We hope you'll come along. We need your advice and input. Judy's making us a supper, so don't eat any dinner. The restaurant suppers are tasty.'

'I'll pop along at seven and we'll talk then,' Abby assured her.

After the call, Josh wandered back over to Abby.

'Some of the quilting bee ladies are meeting in Judy's bar restaurant to chat about selling their quilts and making the website,' she explained.

72

'I'd better let you go then. You've a busy night ahead of you. But I hope you'll come back soon and have tea again.' His beautiful eyes gazed at her.

'Yes, I'd like to.'

He helped her fold the two quilts she was taking away with her and carried them downstairs.

Outside, he walked with her to her car. She put her quilts and bag in the back, and placed Minnie's map on the passenger seat.

Josh smiled. 'Just follow the map backwards this time.'

'It should be easy,' she lied.

Josh waved her off. 'Enjoy your evening — and tell Minnie I'd love to have kissed you, but I didn't have the nerve to ask.'

Abby gasped and blushed all the way to the bluebell niche.

CHAPTER SEVEN

Abby wore the tea dress to the bar restaurant. She had her laptop with her in a shoulder bag, and made her way through the main area where people were having dinner or drinks. Music filtered through from a social event that was starting in the function room. The doors were closed and Abby couldn't see what it was, but the music sounded cheery.

The quilting bee ladies were having their meeting in a room at the back of the premises, and Judy waved to Abby to come through.

Several bee members were there including Minnie and Pearl.

'You look lovely in your tea dress,' said Minnie, as Abby walked over to the large table where they were all seated ready to chat and have supper.

Abby sat down between Minnie and Pearl while Judy busied herself organising the supper with members of staff.

'Is that the dress you wore for your afternoon tea with Josh?' Pearl asked. Pearl wore a top and skirt combo in heather tones.

'Yes, Judy kindly gave me two dresses and I wore this one.' Abby gave a thankful smile to Judy who was wearing a cherry red jersey dress with a swishy knee–length hemline. She'd made it herself and had a penchant for vibrant red and fuchsia colours.

Judy smiled at Abby and placed a large plate of crusty bread slices down on the table. There was white farmhouse bread, rustic and some topped with oatmeal, along with pats of butter.

'How did things go between you and Josh?' Minnie sounded keen to hear all about it.

Abby summarised what had happened while Minnie and the other women listened. She ended by telling Minnie that Josh overheard their conversation.

Minnie laughed. 'He heard me asking if he kissed you?'

'Yes, I was so embarrassed, and then he said he'd wanted to kiss me but didn't have the nerve to ask.'

The women were buzzing with excitement.

'I knew there was a romance brewing,' said Judy. 'Has he asked you out on a date?'

'No, but he said he hopes I'll go back up to house again for tea,' Abby replied.

Minnie clapped her hands with glee. 'Oh, this sounds promising.' She looked at Pearl for her reaction to the budding romance.

'It's about time Josh found himself a nice young woman to have fun with,' said Pearl.

The women laughed, reading more into Pearl's comment than was there.

'Och, you know what I mean. A proper girlfriend,' Pearl clarified.

But the women were giggling and laughing, and the atmosphere in the room was filled with light–hearted banter.

'Is vegetable and chicken stew okay for you?' Judy asked Abby. 'Or would you prefer something else?'

'Stew would be great,' said Abby, feeling hungry. After her visit with Josh she hadn't eaten anything so as not to spoil her appetite as Minnie had suggested.

Plates of the hearty stew with mashed tatties topped with a knob of butter were served up piping hot.

'Tuck in,' Judy told them. 'I'll organise the tea and be back in a tick.'

'So, did you agree to go up to his mansion again?' Minnie asked Abby. 'Did you set a date?'

'Nothing set, but I said I'd like to,' Abby explained.

'I'm sure he'll make a date with you soon,' said Minnie.

Judy came through with a large pot of tea and put it down on the table. A member of staff brought in a second pot. Judy sat down and joined the ladies.

'This stew is tasty,' said Abby.

'Help yourself to the bread,' Judy encouraged her. 'With all the excitement you've probably not eaten anything proper all day except cake with Josh.'

This was true. Abby picked a slice of bread to enjoy with her supper.

'What's going on next door?' Pearl asked Judy. Scottish music played in the background but it was the raised voices that Pearl was concerned about.

'Ceilidh practice.' Judy rolled her eyes. 'Jock's teaching some of the local men a few moves for the ceilidh dancing. Two of them turned up without their kilts and Jock's having none of it.'

'It sounds like argy–bargy,' said Minnie.

Jock's forceful voice sounded through to them. 'I told you, Euan, no kilt, no dance lesson.'

The women tucked into their stew and listened to the men's conversation.

Euan's reply was mumbled, as if he was in a huff, so the women couldn't quite hear what he was saying.

Jock responded loud and clear. 'Breaking your buckle is no excuse, Euan. No, nope. You could've pinned it. So get yourself up those stairs and I'll let you borrow one of mine. You too, Shawn. I know you've been working the farm all day, but we've all been busy, including being out in the fishing boats, so you get your tail upstairs as well. Hurry up the pair of you.'

Minnie glanced at Abby.

Shawn? Abby mouthed to her.

Minnie looked excited and delighted. 'Maybe we'll get a wee peek at them.' She glanced hopefully at Judy.

A mischievous grin lit up Judy's face. 'Yes, we'll wait until they're in full swing and sneak a peek through the serving hatch.'

This plan was met with approval from the other ladies.

There was more mumbling from the function room, followed by Jock's authoritative voice overriding everything. 'You were all well warned. You can't learn ceilidh dancing in trews. You need to feel the birl of your kilt and how your sporran reacts when you're whirling round the dance floor. You have to wear a kilt if you want to get your birling on.'

And that appeared to be the argument over.

Loud clumping was heard as three sets of men's footsteps sounded up the stairs above the back room.

Judy nudged Abby. 'When it comes to kilts, Jock's wardrobe is the equivalent of mine with my dresses. Euan and Shawn will be well kitted out.'

'Is there something special happening that they need to learn ceilidh dancing?' Abby asked Judy.

'We've got a lot more ceilidhs in the community than ever. They've become very popular these past few years. Not all the men know the steps. They can manage to jig at a party or waltz at a wedding, but it's hard to learn ceilidh dancing at an actual dance because it's so fast moving. So, with the run of ceilidhs coming up, Jock decided to give them free lessons on nights when the function room was empty. My Jock know all the dances,' she added proudly.

Abby remembered seeing a ceilidh poster on the wall of the bar restaurant.

'It's Euan's turn to erect a marquee in his field for the forthcoming ceilidh,' Judy continued. 'So that's why he's brushing up on his dancing.'

Minnie chimed–in. 'You'll be joining in of course, Abby. It's in the field beside your cottage. The farmers take turns to host them. Jock organises the events. He's in charge of all the farmers' ceilidh schedules.'

Abby nodded and tucked into her stew wondering about how close to her cottage a wild night of dancing was going to be.

Kitted out but still complaining, Euan trundled down the stairs along with Shawn and Jock.

'I feel like a clootie dumpling in this big kilt,' Euan moaned.

'Awe, wheesht!' Jock scolded him. 'With you being so tall, I had to give you my biggest kilt to cover your knees so you can experience the full swish of the pleats.'

Euan adjusted the large kilt pin on the waistband.

'Stop footering with your kilt, Euan,' Jock told him. 'I've pinned it secure so it'll not let you down.'

Euan said no more, and the doors to the function room were closed as the music was turned up and the lesson began.

Judy dabbed her lips and put her napkin down. 'That's our cue, ladies.'

Keeping quiet, the women followed Judy and made their way over to the serving hatch.

Before sliding it open, Judy put her finger to her lips. 'Remember, not a word. We don't want them to know we're having a wee peek.'

Abby found herself nodding along with the others and feeling the need to be stealthy.

Judy slid the hatch open quietly in a well–practised manner. The women leaned close and viewed the scene.

It was far more entertaining than Abby had anticipated.

Cupping their hands over their mouths to muffle their giggles, the women peeked in on the men.

Jock's teaching methods were interesting. 'I've always believed in throwing folks in at the deep end when they want to learn something fast. So...let's tackle the Eightsome Reel.'

Josh knew he was going to be late. He'd turned back once, and then decided to force himself to be more sociable. Checking local events, he'd noticed the ceilidh lessons for the guys at Jock's function room. Josh could dance, of sorts. He wasn't a complete beginner, but brushing up on his techniques seemed sensible especially as there were a few ceilidh events coming up.

He wore his kilt. The dark grey and black tones suited his styling, and his legs looked fit in his knee length wool socks and brogues. His cropped black jacket emphasised his broad shoulders narrowing down to a lean torso. Under his jacket he wore a white shirt open at the neck and a grey waistcoat. Jock had stipulated kilts were required or no entry.

Believing this sounded like a well–organised lesson, especially as Jock was known as a cheery but no nonsense man, Josh thought this was the ideal evening to start being more social on the local scene.

Unfortunately it clashed with Abby's night with Judy and the ladies, but as the function room was separate, he decided to go and hope she didn't see him. Or if she did, it would help establish he wasn't such a lone wolf and was willing to mix and not sit up in his mansion alone working or training.

The lights of the bar restaurant shone a warm welcome as he headed along the shore road. He took a deep breath. He could do this, he could. Even if it was only to be able to dance with Abby at the forthcoming ceilidhs, it was worth the effort and possible embarrassment.

Josh walked through the busy bar restaurant, causing a few people to stare in surprise. No one said anything to him directly, though he heard their whispered comments. He walked on, opened the doors to the function room and looked in.

Jock saw him and beckoned him to join them. He was taken aback to see Josh there, but made no fuss and offered a smile to welcome him.

'In you come, Josh. We're just warming up our sporrans with an Eightsome Reel. Join in.'

And he did.

Despite a few surprised looks, including from Euan, Josh was soon in full swing dancing with the others. He was quite good too, better than most. He'd attended ceilidhs since he was a boy. Although not properly learned, the dances and steps were familiar enough for him to adapt. The light–footedness of his boxing days came in handy when he had to alter his steps to keep up with Jock.

'Well done, Josh. That was a great turn,' Jock shouted, encouraging him. 'You too Shawn. And Euan, well, keep going.'

Euan did keep going, spurred on by the arrival of Josh. They weren't rivals as such, but Euan had heard about Josh and Abby getting cosy at the mansion, and this made him want to challenge him.

Unaware that he was being challenged, Josh tried to learn the steps. As with everything he'd done in his fight training, he focussed on the movements. When he made a mistake, he'd try again harder, until he got it right. This made him stand out from the other men, but seemed to raise everyone's game and the lesson proved to be hotting up into quite a competitive mode.

Jock kept the pace going, pleased that the lads were giving it their all.

As the music changed, so did the dance, this time to another fast–moving reel.

'Keep going lads,' Jock shouted encouragingly. 'The quickest way to learn is to dance.'

The music was lively and upbeat, creating an uplifting atmosphere, and soon they were all throwing their inhibitions aside and laughing as they danced.

'Give it laldy!' Jock cheered, enjoying himself more than he'd anticipated.

And there at the serving hatch were the faces of several women, watching the men whirl round in their kilts. That's when the trouble began, because in his effort to whirl, Shawn's kilt flew up to reveal he'd opted for the tradition of wearing nothing underneath it.

Minnie yelled, 'Oh, did you see that!' before Judy could nudge her to be quiet.

Even over the music, the women's gasps and giggles were heard. Jock stopped dancing, put his hands on his hips and looked right at the ladies.

'I think we've got a few eyeballs on us, lads,' Jock announced.

The men paused, realising they had an audience.

A couple of the women went to run away, laughing, but Jock called out, 'Oh, no, I saw you.' He strutted over. 'There's penance for peeking, ladies. So get yourselves through here. Two dances with the lads is required. They need to practise dancing with a partner, so hurry through. Come on.'

Clearly Jock wasn't taking no for an answer, and with Judy encouraging the women to pop through for a couple of dances, Abby found herself facing Josh for the Gay Gordons.

Minnie buttoned the lilac cardigan she was wearing over a blouse and skirt. She blushed as she held hands with Shawn. He'd made sure she partnered up with him.

'If you spy on people, you sometimes see things you're not supposed to,' Shawn said to her. This made her blush even more.

But there was little time for conversation as Jock wanted to keep the energy of the dancing in full swing, and soon Abby was dancing with Josh thinking that she'd never lived such a fast–paced life, not even when she worked to tight deadlines at the ad agency. Life here was non–stop.

Another latecomer joined in — Gordon, kilted and ready to dance.

'Sorry I'm late, Jock, but I've just finished at the tea shop,' said Gordon.

'I'm glad you made it, Gordon,' Jock told him, happy his dance lesson night was so popular.

Judy was a skilled dancer and did her best to help Euan improve. And he had.

'You're doing well, Euan,' said Judy, crossing arms with him and leading him when he went awry.

'I thought the lesson would be slower,' Euan said to her.

'Jock's methods work better,' Judy assured him. 'You've got the hang of a few of the dances now.'

Euan beamed, pleased with himself. 'Yes, I'm enjoying them too. It's a fair workout.' He glanced at Josh. 'Although he's barely out of breath,' he gasped.

'Och, don't compare yourself to Josh. We'd all be as fit as him if we galloped along the shore every day. Besides, you've still got the puff to talk to me, so you're fine and fit yourself, Euan.'

'As are you, Judy,' Euan replied.

'Jock keeps me on my toes.' She smiled at Euan and then looked over at her husband and gave him an acknowledging nod.

'Are Josh and Abby dating now?' Euan asked her.

'Not yet, but maybe,' said Judy.

Gordon cut–in as the dance changed again. 'My turn to dance with Judy.'

She was happy to partner with Gordon and everyone changed partners, including Abby and Josh.

At one point Abby had to dance with Euan.

'I'm sorry for everything, Abby,' Euan said as they swirled around.

Abby smiled at him and nodded. Apology accepted, and the air cleared between them. And then they danced on together, until she came full circle back to partner again with Josh.

The two dances sprawled into four, maybe five, probably more. Abby wasn't sure because one dance merged into the next. But she was having so much fun dancing with Josh, and with the others when they changed to dance another Eightsome Reel, that she didn't care. She was a fair ceilidh dancer, having learned as a girl and attended a few functions that included jigs and reels, and Hogmanay parties.

'This is fun,' Josh said, smiling at Abby. He looked so handsome and happy as they held hands and whirled around the dance floor.

'Yes,' she said. 'It's great. I'm so glad I decided to move here to enjoy a quiet life in a cottage by the sea.'

Josh laughed, and as the music picked up pace again, the two of them lost themselves to the warm–hearted company and fun of the dancing.

Judy finally called a happy halt to the ladies dancing.

'We're going to have to leave you lads,' Judy told them. 'We've quilting bee business to chat about.'

Waving them off, the men cheered and applauded.

Judy led the ladies back through to the private room where she organised cool drinks for them.

Abby and the others flopped down on their chairs, exchanging smiles, gossip and breathless laughter.

'I didn't expect to see Josh here,' said Minnie.

Pearl was still astounded. 'He's never been to any local events.' She looked at Abby. 'You've certainly caused a change in him.'

'What was he saying to you?' Minnie asked Abby. 'The two of you were chattering non–stop while you were jigging.'

'Nothing special. Just saying how much fun we were having,' said Abby.

'Has Josh asked you out on a date?' Judy asked her.

'No, not yet,' Abby replied.

'Euan wanted to know if the two of you were dating,' Judy told Abby.

Abby frowned. 'Really?'

'Uh–huh,' said Judy. 'I knew there was romance and trouble brewing.' She looked at Minnie. 'And what about you and Shawn? I've never seen you blush like that in years.'

'I wasn't blushing,' said Minnie. 'I was flushed from the dancing.'

The women laughed, and then so did Minnie.

'Okay,' Minnie relented. 'But I kept thinking about...well...his kilt reveal.'

'Yes, that was a surprise,' added Judy.

'I hope I didn't spoil Jock's class by yelling out like that and causing us to dance with them,' said Minnie.

Judy grinned. 'Are you kidding? The men loved every minute of it, and learned to dance.'

Pearl confided in them. 'I heard Jock say that all the men are commando under their kilts, not just Shawn.'

'I wish you hadn't said that,' Abby commented to Pearl. 'Josh asked if he could walk me home tonight, and I told him yes.'

Judy laughed wickedly. 'Now you'll be hoping the sea breeze picks up as he walks you back along to your cottage.'

'I will not,' said Abby, and then she burst out laughing.

Teasing Abby, they continued to laugh and sipped their cool drinks.

Abby held up her glass, realising she didn't even know what she was drinking. It tasted lovely and refreshing and she'd downed half of it without thinking. She wasn't much of a drinker, and started to feel the effect of it.

'What's in this, Judy?' Abby asked.

'A potent mix. A special cocktail Jock and I concocted — whisky, brandy and fruit juice.'

'Mainly whisky,' Minnie added.

Judy smiled at Abby. 'Two of these and you won't need a sea breeze to find out what's underneath Josh's kilt.'

Abby gasped, and the laughter continued until Jock knocked through to them.

'Behave yourselves through there ladies. We're trying to get our jig on.'

This caused the women to roar with laughter and further knocking through from Jock.

When their joint shenanigans finally subsided, the women chatted about their business plans.

Abby showed them the photographs she'd taken at Josh's house and garden.

Pearl was astounded. 'You got Josh to hold up your quilts for the photos?'

'Yes, he offered to help,' Abby told Pearl.

Minnie had her eye on one of the other pictures Abby showed them on her laptop. 'It's the silk sheets on Josh's bed that I'm looking at.'

This made all the women peer at Josh's bed, and then more teasing was cast at Abby.

'You never mentioned you were in his bedroom,' Minnie said to Abby. 'No, you left that juicy detail out.'

'Minnie!' Abby said giggling.

As they continued to chat about the quilt photos and made their plans for similar pictures, the music from next door slowed down and the men took a break.

They drank chilled glasses of beer at the function room bar. Gordon handed a glass to Josh as they were served up.

Josh wasn't a beer drinker, but a cold, refreshing drink was welcome, and it made him feel part of the company.

Gordon tipped his glass against Josh's. 'Cheers. Here's to you and Abby.'

'I haven't asked her out yet,' said Josh.

'No, but you will.'

Josh couldn't deny this.

'Just don't break her heart, Josh,' Gordon added.

'That's the last thing I want to do.'

CHAPTER EIGHT

At the end of the evening at the bar restaurant the quilting bee ladies had made some firm plans for selling their quilts and decided on a theme for their website.

Abby closed her laptop. Amid all the dancing, laughter and a delicious supper, they'd managed to make progress with their plans. They'd agree to take photographs of their quilts and get together again the following day to select their pictures for the website. Although the quilts were different types and patterns, they wanted to create an appealing presentation of them on the website with each quilter's work displayed to advantage while still complementing the homely but stylish sewing theme. Any costs for the running of the website were minimal enough to be covered by the quilting kitty, the small fund the ladies had for their bee membership.

'I'm going to start by putting four of my quilts up for sale,' said Minnie. 'If the sun's out tomorrow, I'll take photos of them outside in my garden, and as you suggested, Abby, a few inside my cottage. My phone takes great pictures.' Minnie lived in a cottage near her grocery shop that had a small but well tended garden.

Abby had advised the women to set up an area of their house to photograph their quilts for a homely look — and then take pictures of the quilts outdoors in their garden, by the sea or countryside. An outdoors element was going to be part of their presentation to show the colours of the fabric in natural light and utilise the beauty of the fields, flowers and seashore.

Most of them planned to use their phones to take pictures of their quilts and then send the images to Abby along with the measurements and fabric details so she could write the descriptions for them.

As they were getting ready to leave the bar restaurant, they spoke to Gordon and arranged a time to take pictures in his tea shop the following afternoon. He was pleased to be involved and planned to set up tea and cakes for them.

The evening had been a success and full of pleasant surprises including the ceilidh dancing.

'Thanks for the supper, Judy,' said Abby. 'I had a nice time.'

'We managed to get some work done amid all the shenanigans.' Judy eyed Josh and winked at Abby. 'Speaking of which...there could be more of that to come for you tonight. You may end up kissing him after all.'

'Judy!' Abby said in a hushed tone, while trying not to giggle.

Josh was waiting at the door to walk Abby home.

Her heart quickened seeing him standing there looking so handsome in his kilt.

'I'll drop your delivery of cakes off in the morning,' Abby said quickly to Minnie.

'Enjoy your walk home, and don't do anything I would do,' Minnie whispered.

'And what would that be, Minnie?' Shawn said over her shoulder.

Minnie looked round at him. 'Nothing, we were just talking about—'

'Quilting,' Abby cut–in.

Minnie smiled and nodded. 'Yes, exactly.'

Shawn leaned down. 'I can always tell when you're spinning me a line, Minnie.'

Minnie's cheeks flushed. 'I'm sure I don't know what you mean.'

Shawn grinned at her. 'Oh, I'm sure you do. Goodnight, Minnie, and thanks for the dancing. Maybe we can go to one of the ceilidhs? Euan's having a ceilidh soon.'

Minnie was taken aback by his invitation. 'Go with you?'

Shawn nodded.

Minnie tried to contain her delight. 'Yes, I think I'd maybe, probably, sort of like that.'

'Fine then. That's a date,' said Shawn. 'The next ceilidh, it's you and me for a night out at the dancing.'

He smiled at her again and walked away. He'd changed into his own clothes and given the borrowed kilt back to Jock.

Minnie stared at Abby. 'Did I just agree to a date with Shawn?'

'Yes, you did,' said Abby, smiling at her.

Pearl overheard what happened and joined in the conversation. 'Don't do anything Judy would do,' she joked with Minnie.

Judy laughed, hearing the comment. 'Definitely not, Minnie. You need to behave yourself, especially with Shawn. That's a whole lot of man to handle.'

The women's banter and giggling attracted the attention of Jock as he went by, clearing some of the glasses from the tables and putting them on the bar at the end of the night.

'What mischief are you ladies up to now?' Jock asked.

'Nothing,' said Judy, barely hiding her smile.

Abby joined in. 'We were just talking about Minnie and—'

'Quilting,' Minnie cut–in, giving Abby a knowing look.

Jock smiled and shook his head. 'You're all nothing but trouble, especially you, Judy,' he added, grinning at his wife.

Judy smiled at him. 'But you love us anyway.'

'Indeed I do,' said Jock, and continued clearing up the bar.

Abby bid goodnight to the ladies and headed over to Josh at the front door.

Josh smiled at her. 'Causing trouble?'

'No,' said Abby. 'Definitely not.'

Josh smiled again at her, then glanced outside. 'There's a fair breeze blowing along the shore. You may want to put your cardigan on.'

Pearl walked past at that moment on her way out and grinned at Abby. 'Yes, it's a windy night out there.'

Abby tried not to laugh as Pearl walked on.

Josh frowned at Abby for an explanation, but she pretended to be busy putting her cardigan on.

Josh then held the door open for her and they both headed out.

The breeze had picked up and it wasn't just Josh's kilt that was in danger of being blown up by the gusts of wind. Abby's tea dress fluttered in the breeze and she kept smoothing in down to hide her modesty.

By the time they'd reached the shore road the wind was sweeping in from the sea and hitting Abby and Josh in wild gusts.

Clutching tight to her bag and the hem of her dress, Abby forged on, but then she almost stumbled when she stepped on a rut in the grass, and Josh was quick to steady her.

'There's a storm coming in from the sea,' he said. His voice was buffeted by the wind.

She brushed her hair back from her face where the strands whipped across her cheeks, and now flecks of rain were threatening to become another downpour.

Knowing the weather well, and that the rain could start in moments, Josh lifted Abby up in his strong arms and ran with her the rest of the way home to her cottage. It wasn't that far, but far enough for him to think it was safer to get her home than risk getting caught in the storm.

Abby held tight to her bag and put her arm around Josh's shoulder. Beneath the fabric of his jacket she felt the strength of his muscles carrying her with ease to the front door of her cottage.

She didn't object to his help, and it was clear by the way she put her arm around his neck that she was glad of his assistance.

As he put her down the rain started to pour.

She unlocked the door quickly and stepped inside, leaving Josh standing in the brunt of the storm.

In that moment she wondered what to do. Should she invite him to come in and shelter? Or would this seem like an invitation for a lot more than that? She certainly wasn't the type to rush into any casual relationship, and didn't want to give that impression.

Josh understood her predicament.

'It's okay, Abby,' Josh assured her, reading her conflicting expression. 'I'll head home and be there in a few minutes. Lock your door against the storm. Thanks for everything, including the dancing. I don't remember the last time I had so much fun.' He looked at her with caring and longing for a moment.

And then he ran off into the rain, a strong, fit kiltie, and a gentleman she thought.

Josh's heart pounded as he ran home, not from the exertion, but from the feelings welling up inside him thinking about Abby.

His kilt was soaked and the weight of the wet fabric slapped against his bare thighs, making the run harder with every stride. But he didn't care. The kilt would dry, and so would he, but wondering what to do about his feelings for Abby pressed heavily on his shoulders.

He remembered what Gordon had said. *'Just don't break her heart, Josh.'*

This wasn't his intention, though he realised from past experiences that love didn't always accommodate his well–meaning plans. He needed to think things through, and decide what was best for Abby. She had joked about not having time to settle into the cottage for the whirlwind of events and invitations. And she was right. Perhaps he should give her the time she needed? Then again, he'd seen the way Gordon had looked at her, and sensed a streak of rivalry from Euan. If he stepped back, would either of them step forward? It was feasible, and Abby might think that his feelings for her weren't steady.

As the rain poured down the narrow pathway leading to his house, he powered on, deciding to sleep on making a decision.

At the top of the path when he reached the house, he blinked against the rain, wondering whose car was parked in his driveway.

Then he recognised the vehicle as he ran closer.

His heart lurched. What was Keera doing here?

Abby hung her dress up, put on cosy nightwear, and flicked the kettle on for a cup of tea.

She blamed the effects of the potent cocktails for the stirrings in her heart. It was a feeble excuse and she knew it, but admitted the strong attraction she felt towards Josh was quite overwhelming. Yes, she'd made a few mistakes on the dating scene, however, her feelings for Josh were different. Of course he was handsome, but he was also strong yet vulnerable, and clearly trying to be more social. She liked him and sensed that he liked her too. But she'd been wrong about men before...so very wrong.

Pearl had let slip a few secrets about Josh's past relationships earlier in the evening...

'Josh wouldn't like me to tell you this but...' Pearl had then gone on to elaborate... 'I never would've thought he'd come here to the dancing. He's either away on business, busy working at home, or prefers keeping out of the hub of the community. Now, here he is, dancing with you, Abby. I'm delighted for him. His last girlfriend...well...I don't like saying anything about any young lassie, but that one was a right wee madam. Thought the world owed her a living, constantly needed admired and attention. She used to come to visit the mansion and barely spoke a word to me even when I served her meals. No manners and yet a wee snooty nose. I don't know why

Josh dated her. Sometimes I thought he didn't initiate things, and that she was the one chasing him and he was a fool to put up with her. But she was spoiled and used to getting her own way. I was glad, and so were the other staff, when she shouted at him one day that she was never coming back and that they were over. That was several months ago. Thankfully she never came back. She was a model and going into business with her own line of fashion designs.'

Abby drank her tea and gazed out the living room window at the storm.

Mulling over the type of girlfriend Josh had been involved with made her wonder about his interest in her.

She did like him. Apart from being attracted to him, she enjoyed his company. They'd had a lovely afternoon together and then fun at the dancing. If it hadn't been for the rain storm would they have chatted and made further plans as he walked her home to the cottage? The storm cut short what might have been. But she'd never forget his power and strength as he'd lifted her up and ran with her. Or the look he'd given her before leaving.

Keera rolled down the car window and spoke to Josh. 'I've been waiting for over an hour,' she complained. 'There's no staff to let me into the house.' She eyed the state of him. 'Where have you been? And what's with the kilt?' Her pert nose crinkled in disapproval at his soaking kilted appearance.

He pressed his hands on the car, feeling the rain pound his shoulders, and leaned down to talk to her via the open window. No invitation to come in or explanation for what he was doing. He didn't owe Keera any explanation. He didn't owe her anything.

'What do you want?' His words were blunt. No elaborate questions of what she was doing there. If Keera was at his house there was only one reason — she wanted something. Instinct and past experience of being burned by even the slightest request of what Keera ever wanted made him cut out any pleasantries.

Keera sighed and flicked her coiffed chestnut hair with a manicured hand.

'I know we parted on unfriendly terms,' she began.

He interrupted right away. 'Unfriendly? Throwing my laptop from the top storey lounge on to the concrete patio doesn't begin to define how unfriendly your parting shots at me were when I told you we were over.'

'I told you we were finished,' she insisted.

He was tempted to argue, but didn't care enough. 'Why are you here?' he asked her, meeting her cold blue gaze with a stone hard expression.

Rain dripped from his face, but he'd lost none of the handsomeness that had first attracted her to him — and his money.

She could tell by the tone of his voice and flash of resentment in his unwelcoming eyes that she'd have to work hard to persuade him to help her. Taking a deep breath, she decided to be honest.

'I need money.'

Josh didn't even blink.

'My fashion business is in financial trouble. I can handle it, but I need to settle up a few debts this month with the bank. It's the timing. Once I've cleared these silly debts, I can sort out things out from there.'

'What are you not telling me?'

She swallowed her irritation that he could see through her wiles. He always had. Maybe that's what she'd liked about him. Love was too strong a word to use. She'd not fallen deeply in love with Josh, but he was the nearest she'd come to being happy and content. Sadly, she'd then turned her attention to her wealthy business partner, Peter. Mixing business with pleasure worked fine to begin with, but since recently splitting up with Peter, he'd withheld his money from her as well as his affection.

'I split up with Peter.'

Josh wasn't interested.

'He's being awkward and withholding the money I need for this month's payments. The bank won't help me unless I can make a substantial payment. I will have the money from sales I've negotiated, but not in time to deal with this...sticky situation.'

'Why is that my problem?' Josh understood her issues. This made him sure he was the last resort for her to borrow money.

She threw her most kittenish smile at him.

'Don't,' he said. 'I'm not interested.'

She sighed and told him straight. 'Okay, so it's not your problem. Apart from the money, I need you to look over my accounts and financial plans. Peter took care of those, but he's left

91

me to get on with it. I don't have the accounts with me. They're in my office in Glasgow. I trust you. If you'd help me until I find a financial manager that would be great. If not, I could face financial ruin.' She paused and sighed again. 'I just thought that with us having been close in the past you might help me out this one last time before I disappear from your life for ever.'

'Is that a promise?' He couldn't have been clearer.

She nodded. 'Yes.'

'How much money do you need?'

She handed him a piece of paper with the amount shown. 'I'll pay you the money back later when—'

Josh shook his head. He'd rather kiss the money goodbye if it guaranteed he'd never have to deal with her again. He wasn't so cold–hearted to refuse to help her. She was the biggest fool to herself, and in the past, to him. But everyone makes mistakes in business. He could sort hers out. The amount wasn't too much and he could easily afford it.

'Please, Josh,' she cried, thinking his shake of the head was a no. 'I just need—'

'I don't want you to pay me back. I'll give you the money on one condition. That's it. No more. And we're over. You can't come back here again. I have my own life now.'

She nodded. 'Yes, I promise.'

He nodded firmly and walked towards the house. He opened the front door and was about to step inside when she shouted to him through the rain.

'Umbrella!'

He glanced back over his shoulder at her demand for an umbrella so she could enter his house.

There were umbrellas in the hall cupboard. He picked one up and took it out to her.

The minute he gave her the umbrella, he knew it was a mistake.

He should never have let her near the mansion. He should've made her wait in her car while he changed into dry clothes and went back out.

She wore heels so high they made her totter as she hurried in her tight skirt suit towards the mansion. The umbrella blew inside out before she could wrestle it the right way, causing her hair to get wet.

As she stepped into his house she cast the damaged umbrella down on the hall floor, bent forward and shook the rain from her shoulder–length hair.

Timing her movements carefully so Josh saw her as he ran up the stairs, she threw her head back like the fashion model she used to be before embarking on a business career in designer clothes.

A sly smile played on her luscious lips.

He bounded up the stairs, wishing he'd told her to drive off and hadn't taken pity on her. Damn her!

He raised his hand and called down to her. 'Don't come up. Wait there. I'll get changed and be back down.'

He knew his command had as much success as telling an untrained puppy not to jump on the couch.

Tottering stiletto shoes aside, Keera was up those stairs and after him in seconds.

She was hot on his heels and followed him into his bedroom.

He blocked that move immediately. 'No, wait in the lounge.'

She gave him a skittish glance, and then strutted out.

Moments later Josh heard voices sound outside his bedroom door. He'd put on a pair of dark trousers but was still bare–chested and drying his hair with a towel as he went out to see what was going on.

A male member of his staff was talking to Keera. The man recognised her and was obviously taken aback to see her there, and even more so when he saw Josh.

'I'm sorry to interrupt, Josh,' the man said, 'but I was worried the storm would cause damage to the house, so I popped up to check that the patio doors and balcony doors were closed and secure. I thought you were out.'

'I was, and I'm just leaving again. I appreciate you taking care of the property and hope you'll keep an eye on things until I get back,' said Josh.

'Will you be gone long, sir?'

'No, I need to go to Glasgow on business. I'll call tomorrow and let you know my schedule,' Josh explained.

And all the while Keera stood there looking like she was happy with Josh, and giving the wrong impression of the situation.

Josh was in no mind to explain things at that moment, and wanted to get out of the house.

Hurrying into his bedroom, Josh threw on a shirt, tie and jacket, picked up an overnight bag he kept packed ready for urgent business trips, and ushered Keera downstairs, leaving the man to check the balconies.

Keera smiled to herself as she watched Josh gather things from his study and stuff them in his briefcase.

Josh shut the case and looked at Keera. 'Let's go.'

She followed him to the front entrance.

'Are we taking your car?' she asked, standing in the shelter of the doorway expecting him to bring the car over so she didn't get wet.

Josh thrust an umbrella into her ungrateful hands. 'No, separate cars. I'll lead, you follow. We're heading for the city.'

'But it's such a stormy night,' she complained. 'Can't we stay here overnight and leave in the morning?'

'No. It'll ease as we head inland. We always get the brunt of it from the sea.'

Realising that Josh wasn't prepared to be cajoled further, she hurried to her car to drive after him. Maybe it was her imagination, but it sounded like the tyres of his car ground angrily on the wet gravel as he started up the engine, before driving assuredly into the night.

As he drove away from the coast, he looked down at the shore. In the distance, through the rain, he saw the lights were on in Abby's cottage. His heart ached that he couldn't drive down and be with her rather have to leave on a thankless trip with a woman from his past. He wanted Abby to be his present and hopefully his future. He'd never felt like that about anyone before.

He continued on, driving up the countryside to where the road led to the nearest town and city beyond. He had to push the thoughts of the ceilidh aside, the images of Abby smiling at him, and holding hands with her at the dancing. Such heart–warming pleasures that money couldn't buy.

Now he was in a situation that money could buy and mend. But the turmoil inside him was as powerful as the storm blowing in from the sea.

Abby snuggled up in bed under her quilt and watched the raging sea release its wrath outside her window. She'd lit a candle in the night light beside her bed, welcoming the warm glow of the flickering flame inside the coloured glass.

The rain and wind battered off the window, but the cottage was built of stern stuff and refused to let the elements in. Abby felt safe and protected, though could she say the same for her heart? Her feelings for Josh put her in jeopardy.

Pushing aside all sensibility, embarking on a romance with a man like Josh was akin to standing outside the cottage and defying the effects of the storm. Of course she was going to risk being buffeted and emotionally windswept.

Leaving her life in the city behind, she thought she'd prepared everything — paperwork, finances, her precious belongings including her quilts, but she hadn't anticipated being dropped into the deep end when it came to romance. Euan was the first jolt of masculine presence and although they'd settled their differences earlier at the dancing, seeing him striding across his field was a memory burned into her thoughts. Then there was warm–hearted Gordon, welcoming her into his tea shop and his life as if she belonged there. And the fit figure of Josh running along the shore, and the sense of him noticing her — that inexplicable connection between two people that only happens a few times in a lifetime. Was she simply out of her depth and not ready for romance? Or was she foolish enough to believe that a man like Josh didn't bring heartache as well as hope and happiness?

She suddenly shivered, hugged her quilt up tight and peered at the waves lashing on to the shore. Something didn't feel right, as if the balance had tilted from her favour — an instinct, a warning to get ready to defend her heart from harm.

Josh glanced in the rearview mirror, catching a last glimpse of the shore before driving on to a main road leading away from the coast. His heart yearned for him to turn around and head back home, and yet he couldn't. The headlights of the car behind him reminded him that Keera was back in his life, if only for a day or two.

He told himself he'd be home again soon after sorting her finances. Then he'd ask Abby out on a proper date.

CHAPTER NINE

Abby was up early the next morning having slept through the storm. Bright sunlight streamed in the kitchen windows, and as the oven heated up from all the cake baking, she opened the kitchen door to let the fresh air in.

The garden looked intensely colourful, and the rain had refreshed everything without causing any damage. Even the rambling roses retained their grip on the shed.

She went outside and brought her bicycle out of the shed ready to pack the basket with her cake delivery for Minnie's shop. The shed was dry inside, and if she hadn't been so busy baking she'd have tried her hand at potting plants and gardening. Things she aimed to make time for.

But right now, there were cakes to be iced, buttercream to whip and orders to be packed for delivery to Minnie and Gordon. She'd also made shortbread for Judy.

Josh had been in her thoughts while she was baking. Even when she was concentrating on the recipes to measure the ingredients and follow the methods, Josh was on her mind. The doubts from the depths of the night had subsided along with the storm. Maybe her heart was in jeopardy, but she was feeling more optimistic as she busied herself with the baking.

Abby had found an extra bicycle basket tucked in a cupboard in the cottage. She'd buckled it on to the back of her bike and filled it with cakes and shortbread. The basket was large enough to hold most of her orders along with using the front basket and a bag slipped over one of the handlebars.

Laden with cakes, she cycled along the shore road to Minnie's grocery store, occasionally glancing up towards the trees that hid Josh's mansion. Was he having breakfast on the balcony and perhaps looking down at her? Would she see him later today? Her afternoon was going to be busy with the quilting bee ladies at Gordon's tea shop, but with their recent closeness it seemed probable Josh would contact her later.

She felt quite fit as she cycled along, and reckoned the energetic ceilidh dancing and frantic bike riding was like a form of training. It wasn't a patch on Josh's running and fight training, shadow boxing or whatever it was he did to keep his muscles strong and taut, but she certainly felt fit and wanted to start swimming. The sea sparkled so enticingly in the morning light, in shades of green from the gem–like glints on the surface to the deep emerald tones that stretched along the bay. In the distance, further along the shore road, she saw a man running towards the sea. For a moment she associated the running figure with Josh, but it wasn't him, it was Gordon, heading for his morning swim. He didn't see her.

She wanted to rejig her schedule to accommodate a morning dip. Once she settled into things, she'd arrange her routine to include swimming. She wondered if Josh went swimming or if running was more his thing. And there she was thinking about Josh again.

By now, she'd reached Minnie's shop, parked her bike outside and carried the cake order in.

Minnie thanked and paid her for the cakes, but was more concerned about the photos of her quilts and thrust her phone at Abby.

'My garden was still a wee bit wet early this morning, but the sun was out and everything was glinting beautifully, so I hung my quilts on the washing line and photographed them with the garden in the background. What do you think? I quite like them. The colours look fresh and my garden's come up quite well.'

Abby agreed. 'They look great. The sunlight shows the colours of the quilts and the garden is lovely.'

Minnie looked proud. 'I tried my best. I took into account all the things you said about the background, not getting poles or stuff like that in the pictures. I know you can crop awkward bits out, but I wanted to take them without you having to do that.'

Abby flicked through the images on Minnie's phone. The four quilts were traditional designs. 'These photos will work. Your quilts are beautiful and it was a great idea hanging them on the clothes line. It shows the designs well.'

'I'll take some pictures of them inside my cottage and of course we've our photos to set up at Gordon's tea shop this afternoon.' Minnie smiled. 'It's so exciting. I know there's no guarantee that I'll sell my quilts, but I'm enjoying our wee venture.'

'There's nothing quite like having fun while you work.' Abby didn't want to get Minnie's hopes up in case things didn't work out, but she was pretty sure she could advertise these quilts so they would sell. She'd had harder assignments than this to handle. These quilts were lovely, they'd be priced competitively, described enticingly but accurately and with pictures like this, she envisioned that customers would want to buy them.

'Was Netta a member of the quilting bee?' Abby asked.

'No, she was a knitter, not a quilter. Netta loved her knitting and her baking. Her cake recipes meant a lot to her,' Minnie explained. 'I think that's why she wanted someone like you to continue them so they wouldn't be forgotten.'

Abby nodded thoughtfully. 'That's what I love about quilts. Each block, each piece of fabric is stitched to last for years.'

Minnie agreed, and then she said, 'The ladies are looking forward to taking pictures of their quilts at the tea shop. Are you bringing yours along?'

'Yes, I'm happy with the photos taken at Josh's house, so I'll bring other quilts to the tea shop.'

'How did things go when Josh walked you home last night?' Minnie asked.

Abby relayed the details. 'The storm caused him to pick me up and run with me to the cottage before the rain became heavy.'

Minnie's eyes widened. 'Oh, how romantic. Did you feel his muscles?'

Abby shook her head. 'No.'

Minnie grinned at her.

'Okay,' Abby relented. 'He's very strong.'

Minnie giggled. 'Did you invite him in for tea or coffee?'

'No, I didn't want to take things too far. He understood and ran off home in the rain.'

'Are you seeing him later today?'

Abby shrugged. 'I'm not sure. Due to the storm, we didn't make any plans.'

'He's bound to want to meet up with you. He'll know you're busy in the morning with the baking, and he probably knows we're at the tea shop this afternoon, so perhaps he'll invite you to his house for dinner.'

Abby's heart soared at the thought of this.

Someone came into the shop and Minnie served them while Abby got ready to leave. Abby bent down and clapped Bracken in his basket and he was happy to nuzzle into her.

'I'll see you at the tea shop, Minnie,' said Abby.

Minnie smiled and nodded.

Abby walked with her bike to the tea shop and stopped outside. Gordon was finishing his quick dip in the sea and making his way back up, drying himself with a towel. He wore red trunks and nothing else. He had a great build and an outdoors look to him.

Striding up to the shop in his bare feet he smiled and waved to her.

'I hope you haven't been waiting long, Abby.'

'No, I've just arrived. I was at Minnie's shop delivering her cakes — and gossiping.'

Gordon grinned at her. 'You've certainly got lots to gossip about. Dancing with Josh last night and then him walking you home. And Shawn making a date to go ceilidh dancing with Minnie.'

'You're quite the ceilidh dancer yourself, Gordon.'

'I enjoy the ceilidhs. It's great that Jock's helping us improve our skills, especially with the next ceilidh due soon in Euan's field. Mark your dance card for a couple of reels with me.'

Abby laughed. 'Consider my card marked for at least two.'

Gordon was happy with this. 'Come on in.' He grabbed one of her bags of cakes and carried it into the tea shop.

She stepped inside carrying the rest of the order.

'If you don't mind, could you put the order in the kitchen while I pop up and get changed?' he asked.

'Yes. Don't rush. I'll sort the cakes out,' she said, heading into the kitchen. She caught a glimpse of Gordon's leanly muscled body as he bounded up the stairs, and mentally scolded herself for peeking. Yes, Gordon was fit. Not like Josh, but to be fair, Josh had trained as a fighter for years. Gordon was a tea shop owner and had a fair physique for a man.

'Put the kettle on for a cuppa if you want,' he called down to her.

'Thanks, I will,' she said, planning to make them both a cup of tea.

The tea shop kitchen smelled delicious. Gordon had been up early as usual baking his own range of cakes, scones, flans and confectionery. The scent of vanilla, strawberry and chocolate filled the air.

He was a tidy worker, and kept his kitchen clean, so she washed her hands and was careful to put her cakes down on the trays and not make a mess.

She flicked the kettle on and set up the cups for tea. He had a selection of teas and she opted for a breakfast tea brew as a refreshing start to the day.

By the time she'd prepared the tea in one of his lovely teapots, Gordon came bounding down the stairs, dressed for work in dark trousers and a clean white shirt. His hair was still damp but he'd brushed it back from his face.

He finished rolling up his sleeves as he breezed into the kitchen.

'I usually have my breakfast after a swim,' he said, firing up the grill for toast. 'Want to join me?'

'You don't need to do that, Gordon. Have your breakfast. I'm happy with a cup of tea. I'll get my breakfast when I get back to the cottage.'

'So, do you like scrambled eggs or beans with your toast?'

Abby laughed. 'Whatever you're having.'

'Scrambled eggs and beans it is.'

He grinned at her and she smiled at him. He was so easy to be around. A lovely man, as Minnie had said when she spoke about Gordon. And she was right.

Abby helped him make the breakfast. They worked well together, as if they'd done this for a while.

'If I'm ever busy, and don't have my part–time staff to help me, I'm phoning you,' he said. 'You look like you've worked in catering for years, rather than an ad agency.'

She buttered their toast. 'I'm happier doing this type of work — baking, and of course quilting.'

Gordon served up the eggs and beans.

Abby poured the tea and then they sat down to eat breakfast.

Gordon stirred milk into his tea. 'So, spill.'

'Spill?'

He picked up his knife and fork and motioned for Abby to reveal the gossip. 'What happened with you and Josh last night? Tell me all the gossip.' He started to eat his breakfast, settling down to enjoy the details.

Abby smiled at him.

'Come on,' he said. 'You know Minnie's going to tell me everything anyway.'

This was true, Abby thought, and began to relay the events of the storm and Josh.

'He carried you to your cottage?' Gordon sounded impressed.

'The rain was getting heavy,' she explained, while tucking into her breakfast.

'I'm sure it was, but I think you could've managed to walk the short distance to your cottage.' He tried to stifle a laugh. 'Good move though from Josh.'

'You think he's making moves on me?' Moves sounded more calculating, like the moves men had made in her past. Her past mistakes. She wanted Gordon's perspective on things.

'Yes. I'm not saying he's being underhand, but he'd know that lifting you up in his arms would bring you closer, and all the heart pounding effect it would have.' He glanced at her. 'You know what I mean.'

She did.

'So you didn't invite him into the cottage?' Gordon asked.

'No, and he didn't take advantage of the situation. He didn't push things further.'

'What if he had?'

She didn't know what to say, because she wasn't sure what she would've done.

Gordon sipped his tea, looking thoughtful. 'You seemed happy dancing with him. You both look like a great couple. But tread warily, that's all I'm saying.'

The thoughts from the previous night returned. The doubts, the feeling that she needed to defend her heart.

'Why do you think I need to do that?' she asked him.

Gordon shrugged. 'Josh is a fine catch.'

Abby jumped in to clarify this. 'I'm not after Josh because he's rich and successful.'

'And handsome,' Gordon added.

'Well, yes, but I'm not the type of woman—'

'I know,' Gordon cut-in. 'I wasn't inferring anything. You haven't chased Josh. He's made all the moves, starting with inviting you to his mansion for afternoon tea. Then he joined in the ceilidh dancing. It's not like him. It's out of character, unless he's simply smitten with you, and that's the most likely explanation.'

'What's the alternative explanation?'

'I don't know. That's why I think you should tread warily. He doesn't have a good track record when it comes to relationships. His last girlfriend wasn't liked by any of the staff at his house, or anyone else I know who met her.' He paused. 'Though I should talk. I'm still single. Maybe he's the same as me — he's never found the right woman to settle down with.'

They continued chatting while eating breakfast, and although the conversation became lighter again, Abby sensed that something wasn't right when it came to Josh. Something had changed. Maybe later on she'd talk to him.

After breakfast with Gordon, Abby dropped off the shortbread to Judy and then headed back to her cottage.

She set up her sewing machine in the lounge and planned to get some quilting done.

With the sun streaming in she began sewing the binding on to one of the bumblebee quilts that was part of her new designs. The bright colours of the bees popped against the solid white background. She'd used a pretty bee print for the backing fabric.

Sitting at her machine, she realised how much she'd missed her quilting. She loved working with fabric and stitching with her sewing machine or by hand. This was what she'd imagined living in the cottage would be like — happily sewing after baking the cakes. The rhythmic whirr of the machine soothed her senses.

She tried not to think about Josh and the well–meaning warning from Gordon to be wary. But even as she concentrated on the stitching, it was hard not to consider the things Gordon had brought up. According to everyone, Josh was acting out of character. Perhaps caution was advisable, at least until she'd had a proper date with him.

Her heart quickened at the thought of dating Josh, becoming involved with someone again. In an ideal world she'd have moved into the cottage, settled into a busy but cosy routine baking and quilting for a few months, and then started to consider dating.

She continued quilting, and then made progress with her own website, adding the photos taken at Josh's house. The pictures of her quilts looked great as she uploaded them to the website, building an attractive selection and writing notes for the descriptions.

She was so busy enjoying her work that she forgot to stop for lunch, and then realised it was time to head along to the tea shop in the afternoon.

With quilts packed into the baskets of her bike, she cycled along, armed with her laptop and pieces of fabric from her stash that she hoped to include in the photos.

Minnie and Judy were heading into the tea shop as Abby arrived on her bike. They were laden with bags full of quilts. Minnie had someone keeping an eye on her grocery shop and Bracken.

They all went inside and started to set up the tables that Gordon had provided. The main tea shop wasn't busy.

'Tea and cakes will be ready soon,' Gordon told them. 'I thought I'd set things up as if it was the quilting bee night. Help yourselves to anything you need to add to the photos. I brought a couple of extra lights down from upstairs in case you needed them.'

'Thanks, Gordon,' said Minnie.

Other ladies arrived, and soon they were busy helping each other take the photos. Gordon had even set up their sewing machines so they could use them as props.

Vintage teapots and floral teacups were used to create a traditional setting, and Abby advised them to drape their quilts on the chairs or hold them up as part of the background.

'Adjust the angles,' Abby said to them. 'Take close–up shots of the stitching and the fabric of the quilts while including a vintage teapot or cup in the picture.'

Abby snapped some pictures to show them how to make the most of capturing their quilts in the tea shop setting. Picking up tips from Abby, the ladies were eager to make their photos interesting while displaying their work to full advantage.

The photo–shoot extended out into the tea shop garden. They took turns at holding their quilts up in the afternoon sunlight.

There was fun and laughter as some of the cakes and scones were eaten while they were taking the pictures.

'Don't worry, Gordon,' Judy assured him, 'we're all paying for the cakes we scoff and the tea.'

Gordon gave Judy the thumbs up and topped up the cake stands with cupcakes and scones.

Minnie sipped a cuppa while chatting to Abby. 'You mentioned that I should sell some of my quilted oven gloves, pot holders and bags, so I've brought a few of those.' Minnie put her cup down and showed her a selection of pretty items.

'These are lovely, Minnie,' said Abby and helped her snap photos of them.

Other members had brought quilted bags they hoped to sell, and Abby advised them on the best way to advertise them along with their quilts.

They included everything from the sewing machines to the cake stands, teapots and cosy scenes by the fireside in their photos, and Abby knew she'd have plenty of great pictures to work with for their website.

'I wonder where Pearl is?' said Minnie. 'She told me she'd be here.'

'She's probably working a bit late at Josh's mansion,' Judy suggested. 'It was her day off yesterday, so she's maybe got extra things to do before she can get away from her work.'

Minnie nodded, and had just helped herself to a butterfly cake when Pearl arrived at the tea shop.

It was clear from Pearl's expression that something was wrong. The women became quiet as she looked awkwardly around the group.

'What's wrong?' Judy asked her. 'Has something happened?'

Pearl took a deep breath. 'I really don't know how to say this, or if I should say it.'

Minnie pressed her. 'Please, Pearl, you've got us all worried.'

Pearl reluctantly relayed the story. 'Last night one of the other staff members went up to Josh's house to make sure the balcony doors were secure from the storm, and found Josh coming out of his bedroom with his top off. Keera, his ex–girlfriend, was there.'

The gathering of women looked to Abby for her reaction.

Abby remained silent for a moment. She felt her world tilting a bit as she adjusted to the new information. Her love life was playing out in her head. Another man she'd misjudged.

'Keera seemed happy,' Pearl elaborated. 'Josh had his overnight bag with him, and they drove off together to Glasgow. That's where Keera lives. He's going to be away with her for a few days.'

Minnie broke the silence. 'Abby, I'm so sorry. Josh has a lot of explaining to do,' she added in a snippy tone.

Abby realised the whole room was holding its breath. 'We weren't dating,' she began with an unconvincing shrug. 'He doesn't owe me any explanation. We weren't involved...' Her words trailed off, and the emotion of the moment overtook her. She wiped a tear from her eye.

Judy put her arms around Abby and hugged her close.

'Oh, this is all my fault,' said Judy. 'If I hadn't made such a big fuss of Josh helping you up that night at the shore, you'd never have given it another thought.'

'It's my fault too,' Minnie added.

Pearl chimed in. 'We all got swept up in the idea of a romance and now you've gotten hurt because of it.'

The women were nodding apologetically.

'No, you weren't doing anything wrong,' Abby insisted. 'You know him. You knew it was unusual behaviour for him. I believe your hearts were in the right place. I'll be fine in a few minutes, really.' Abby went over to finish taking photos of a quilt beside one of the sewing machines.

Gordon brought through a cake stand laden with cream meringues and chocolate éclairs. He noticed the teary look on Abby's face. He whispered to Minnie. 'Is Abby okay? She looks upset.'

'Pearl told us Josh was half–naked coming out of his bedroom last night after he dropped Abby off at her cottage,' Minnie confided. 'Keera was there and they left together for Glasgow. He's going to be away for a few days with his ex–girlfriend.'

Gordon frowned. 'I warned Abby to be careful of getting involved with Josh.'

Minnie looked distraught. 'We're to blame for encouraging her to trust him and egging her on about the romance.'

'Yes, but he looked like he was interested in her. He was so happy dancing with her,' Gordon reasoned.

Minnie shrugged. 'He probably was, until his ex turned up and wanted him to get back together again. Then Abby gets kicked to the kerb.'

Gordon felt upset for Abby. 'Maybe there's another reason for his behaviour.'

'What other explanation could there be?' said Minnie.

Gordon sighed. 'By all accounts, Keera's a manipulative wee vixen. She could've inveigled Josh into running off with her.'

Minnie wasn't convinced. 'Josh was striped to the waist coming out of his bedroom. Keera was there with him. They were alone in the house and not expecting any staff to arrive. Josh then left with a packed overnight bag. Keera was smiling, happy.'

Gordon shook his head, feeling frustrated.

Abby's phone rang. *It's Josh*, she mouthed to Judy. Then she went to the back of the tea shop.

The women and Gordon became quiet.

Abby accepted the call and heard Josh's voice begin to explain...

'I wanted to check in with you, and let you know I'm going to be out of town for a few days.'

His words washed over her like she was numb. She could see the pattern repeating in her love life again, another man lying to her. She'd been down this road before, not again.

Josh continued, 'An old acquaintance needs help with their accounts and managing some loans before the month's end.'

'An old acquaintance, or an old flame, Josh?'

Her words hung in the air for a moment.

'I see the gossip is already circulating around.' His tone was tense.

'Something like that.'

Josh took the hit, feeling he deserved it. 'I'm sorry, Abby, I should have just been straight with you. Keera is an ex.'

Abby jumped in and cut him short. 'You don't owe me any explanation.'

'But I feel that I do. You see, I really wanted to have nothing to do with her again.'

'It's a bit strange then that you ran off with her to Glasgow last night.'

'I didn't run off with her. I did this for you. She turned up at my door and I saw a chance to get her out of my life for good.' His words were becoming strained as he tried to correct his mistake, wishing he could be there to say it to her face so she could see his sincerity. Why wasn't he there? What had he done?

'In what world is this possibly for my benefit?'

'That's not what I mean I...I had such a good time with you at the dancing, and then I came home and she was there. I thought she was going to ruin things, but there was a way I could get her away.'

'I've heard enough,' she said.

Josh's deep voice resonated down the phone. 'I didn't want you to find out like this.'

'In my experience, men generally don't want me to find out at all.' The cutting words were out before she could stop herself.

'Abby, I really want to talk to you in person and explain myself.'

'Well, Josh, if you hadn't run off to Glasgow with your ex, you'd be here in person, but like I said, you don't owe me an explanation. I think we should keep our relationship purely professional from now on.'

She hung up before she cried or said anything else.

The message she'd given to Josh was loud and clear. But Abby didn't want the photo–shoot to become about her troubles with him, so she took a deep breath and went over to join the ladies again.

The women hurried to look like they hadn't been eavesdropping.

'Are you okay, Abby?' Minnie asked.

'Yes, I'll be fine,' said Abby.

Pearl put the thread order down on a table and tried to lighten the atmosphere. 'I picked up the variegated thread from the fabric shop in town.'

Minnie, Judy and others who had ordered it came over for a look.

'They're lovely,' said Minnie, admiring the different tones in the variegated threads she'd asked Pearl to pick up for her.

Abby pushed the feelings from Josh's call aside and took an interest in the thread order. 'This is the blue one I used for the quilt I showed you.' Quite a few of them had ordered this thread.

'I can't wait to try it,' Judy exclaimed. 'I love trying new products.'

Customers came into the tea shop. They'd booked a late afternoon tea. Gordon had their table set at the window.

'Excuse me,' Gordon said to the bee members. 'I have to pipe more cream into my meringues.' And off he went, promising to bring them another pot of tea.

CHAPTER TEN

'Don't be sitting brooding about Josh on your own at the cottage,' Minnie said to Abby as the ladies packed up their things to leave the tea shop. It was late afternoon. Minnie had a part–time helper looking after her grocery shop and was now heading back there. 'There's a function on tonight at Judy's bar restaurant and she says you're welcome to pop along.'

Abby smiled at the offer. The ladies hadn't known what else to do regarding Josh, so the remainder of the afternoon became a happy time taking loads of photos at Gordon's tea shop. 'Thanks, Minnie, but I'm going to get these photos organised and on the website. It'll keep me busy.'

'Well, you know where we are if you need us.' Minnie gave Abby's arm a reassuring squeeze.

A few other members offered a comforting word to Abby as they all headed out, and it made her realise that she'd made some really good friends. This made her even more determined to do a great job of their website.

Gordon handed Abby a bag as she was leaving.

'What's this?' she said, taking a peek.

'A slice of my special cheese and tomato quiche. It's sprinkled with cheddar and greentails. I've also put in a portion of fresh green salad just in case you haven't had a chance to stock up your kitchen with groceries. Apart from items to bake your cakes. Make sure you eat a dinner.' He gave her a look like he knew she'd dwell on thoughts of Josh and may not cook anything proper for herself.

'I appreciate this, Gordon.'

Abby packed her quilts and the dinner bag into the basket of her bicycle and set off down the shore road. The sky hung over the sea, low and ominous, threatening another storm.

The breeze blew through her unbuttoned cardigan as Abby put a spurt on to reach the cottage before it rained. An early twilight had settled over the landscape, and there was a strange energy in the air, or perhaps it was her own deep upset clashing with her determination not to let Josh affect her any longer. From past experience, it wasn't worth the heartache. She'd let her guard down.

Her mistake. And shame on him for being a two–timing rat. Or was he? She'd told the ladies that Josh owed her no explanation for his behaviour. They weren't dating.

She jumped off her bike at the cottage's front garden and wheeled it round the back to the shed. She was starting to love the shed. Old, worn, but sturdy and reliable. It was like a little house in itself. There were even lilac net curtains on the windows tied up with garden twine. The air inside it tonight smelled of apples and maple tree syrup.

The deep roll of thunder resonated across the vast sky above her as she carried her bags from the shed to the cottage.

She glanced up at the stormy grey clouds and hurried inside the kitchen, locking the door against the world.

She flicked on the lamps in the lounge and lit the fire. The cottage soon felt warm and cosy, but she kept the curtains open to watch the storm gathering over the sea.

There was a warm, homely feeling to being in the cottage with the flickering glow of the fire, while putting the kettle on for tea and preparing the dinner Gordon had given her.

Setting up a small table, she ate dinner in the lounge beside the fire.

After dinner she set up her laptop and worked on the quilting bee website and her own business.

Josh looked out the window of his hotel at the lights of Glasgow. Keera had invited him to stay at her house, but he'd booked into a hotel on his own.

He'd worked on Keera's financial mess all day, organising a transfer of funds from his bank to her business account. All matters were dealt with legally and efficiently, but still not quick enough for Josh. He wished he was done sorting out Keera's business and was back home. Not long now though. Whether Abby wanted to let him explain the situation weighed heavily on him.

The sky above the city was stormy, as was his predicament with Abby. She'd sounded angry and disappointed with him. The latter upset him more. Her anger was understandable. They hadn't dated, but they were obviously heading that way, and if Keera hadn't stepped back into his life, he'd probably have been enjoying dinner with Abby. Their first proper date. Instead, here he was wondering if

Abby would ever trust him again, or if he could make things right when he got home.

Abby viewed the progress she'd made with the websites. The photos of the quilts were great and she'd written descriptions of most of them. The ladies had given her the correct sizes and other details, and from these she'd been able to put together informative and interesting pieces of description to complement the images. She'd done this plenty of times for work and quite liked the process.

The storm wasn't as fierce as the previous evening, but it was a night to be in cosy by the fire.

She was working away when she heard noises coming from the back garden. Probably the storm, she thought, then she saw the figure of a man outside.

Flicking off the lamps so she could peer out the patio doors without being lit up, she saw that Euan was in her garden. He looked like he was trying to break into her shed.

Enraged, she hurried out to challenge him. How dare he. Clearly she was still fired up with inner rage at Josh, so Euan was about to be on the receiving end of her ire.

'Your shed door was blowing open,' Euan shouted to her as she stepped outside. 'I think the latch needs tightening.'

Thankfully, she hadn't yelled at him for trespassing, and went over to help.

'I was securing one of my gates and heard your shed door banging in the wind,' he explained. 'I wouldn't have intruded, but I didn't want it damaged.'

By now Euan was tightening the latch.

'I appreciate it,' she said.

The rain felt like icy daggers hitting her face and bare arms. She hugged her arms around her.

'Get back inside, Abby. Keep warm and dry. I'll sort this in a tick.' He motioned for her to leave him to it, so she did.

She ran back inside and watched him from the shelter of the lounge patio. He was wearing a dark green waxed jacket with the collar turned up against the wind and rain. He looked strong and capable, and she was truly grateful for his help. The shed could've been damaged and soaked with the rain.

'There you go,' he said. 'That's it secure.'

'Thanks for doing that, Euan,' she called out to him.

He gave her an acknowledging wave and then jumped back over the fence into his field. Euan's fitness wasn't borne from gym training. Like most of the men she'd met here, their core strength was built from years of outdoor work, creating a hardiness that she secretly found quite manly. Not that she was attracted to Euan, but she could appreciate a fit man like him.

Closing the patio doors, she made herself a hot cup of tea and then settled again beside the fire to continue working on the websites. Once they were up and running, she'd have more time for quilting and other things. Thankfully Judy was happy to update the quilting bee website and had no qualms about doing so. As for her own website, she anticipated sales of her quilts would build slowly, so she wouldn't need to constantly update it with new stock.

The bee website enabled the members to sell their quilts online, and in many ways the community embraced the modern world, and yet...there were things here that were still part of the past, traditional. She loved that the community combined both.

The wind whipped along the shore, and she sipped her tea and enjoyed the heat from the fire.

The box of chocolates from Gordon's tea shop enticed her to have a square of Scottish tablet with her tea. The sugary sweetness melted in her mouth and reminded her of years ago. She hadn't eaten tablet in a long time, but it tasted as she remembered.

Abby stayed up late to get the work done and then climbed into bed, forcing herself to think about quilting rather than dwell on Josh.

When she found her mind drifting to Josh being in Glasgow with his ex, she planned what type of quilt she'd start sewing next. Perhaps one in grey tones that captured the colours of the sea storm, quilted like waves of fabric washing on to the shore...

The morning was deceiving. As Abby cycled along the shore road to deliver her cakes there was no hint of the previous night's storm. No seaweed washed up from the shore, residue of the rain on the grass or brisk breeze. Instead, the sun shone bright in a cobalt blue sky and the breeze felt warm.

Abby wore a white cardigan over her pink top and jeans, but she sensed that summer was well on the way. Yes, there was a definite change in the weather and real heat in the sunshine.

She gazed out at the sea as she cycled towards the shops. If the weather picked up she'd definitely spend days down on the sand and swim in the sea. The water glimmered in the morning sunlight and she longed to go for a swim. The coldness would probably take her breath away, but there was Gordon in the distance enjoying his daily dip. Arguably, he was acclimatised to it and made of sterner stuff than her, but she still longed to enjoy swimming in the sea.

Promising herself that she'd go swimming soon, she made her cake delivery to Minnie's grocery shop. Minnie had been busy serving customers so any talk about Josh had to be shelved. Minnie gave her the sprinkles and other grocery items she'd ordered, and Abby left with those in her basket. She also bought a fresh crusty loaf and a bag of Ayrshire tatties to cook for her dinner later, along with carrots, cabbage, onions and greentails.

Next up was the tea shop delivery. Gordon was still swimming in the sea, but he'd left the door unlocked so she put the Victoria sponges in the kitchen and then went on to Judy's bar restaurant. Judy had messaged Abby asking if they could chat about the new website and so Abby had brought her laptop along. Judy insisted she have breakfast with her.

Over a breakfast of porridge with creamy milk and fresh raspberries and peach slices, Abby showed Judy the quilting bee website.

Judy was impressed. 'That looks well set up and ready for business. You've done us proud.'

'I'm glad you like it.'

'The quilting bee is on again tomorrow night,' said Judy. 'We could launch the website then. Make a special night of it. Press the button and make the items for sale.'

Abby agreed. 'Once the website is live I'll send out emails to potential customers and we'll build things from there.'

'It's so exciting, isn't it,' said Judy. She sipped her tea and then asked, 'Have you heard from Josh? A text message, or an email?'

'No, nothing.' Abby tried to hide her disappointment.

'I was talking to Jock about him last night. He tended to agree with Gordon that Keera may have wangled her way back into his life. Men can be so stupid when it comes to things like that. Keera's got a reputation for being a sneaky wee besom.'

Abby sighed. 'Do you think she's got some sort of emotional hold over him?'

'Jock thinks it'll boil down to money. She wants money, a loan, or help with her finances. Jock met her a few times when she came into the bar for a drink, and he's great at sussing people out. He always thought she was just after Josh's money and that the only person she was interested in was herself.'

'If Jock's right and it is to do with money, surely any transfer of funds could've been done at the mansion. Why would he need to drive off to spend the night with her in the city?'

'That's what I asked my husband and he said it's because it's where she has her business.'

'Josh must have wanted to help her,' said Abby.

'My husband is nobody's fool, but he credits me with being able to bamboozle him when I want to.'

'You're saying she manipulated Josh into helping her?' said Abby.

Judy shrugged. 'They used to date. Perhaps she used their past to wangle his help. Really all I'm meaning is, maybe you should give Josh the benefit of the doubt.'

Abby left Judy's bar restaurant with a lot on her mind. She cycled back to the cottage and put her groceries away. With the morning still early and the full day ahead, she decided to go exploring in the area. A walk outdoors in the sunshine was surely better for her than sitting inside working and dwelling on thoughts of Josh.

She stepped outside the cottage and looked along the length of the bay, shielding her eyes from the dazzling reflections glistening off the sea. At one end were the shops and the harbour, but she'd yet to explore the other direction, so she ventured along to where she'd seen Josh running and disappearing into the trees. As he wasn't anywhere near, she felt free to go venturing up the narrow pathway that led from the shore road to the hillside.

A sense of excitement went through her as she headed into what looked like a secret pathway, overarched with tree branches and edged with bushes and greenery. The sun flickered through the branches, and the air was potent with the scent of the verdant surroundings. Even breathing this in for a few minutes while she picked her way up the well–worn path, felt like aromatherapy for the heart and soul. She understood why Josh liked to use this route because it was a convenient path from his house to the shore, but she thought he must've benefited from the wonderful scent of the trees and plants.

Pausing to explore part of the route, she peered through the greenery and had a great view of Euan's house. This close, the house was bigger than she'd thought, quite substantial in fact, with a garden around the entire property. It wasn't as grand as Josh's mansion, but it was more manageable and without the need for regular staff.

Walking on, she pictured Josh bounding up the path. No wonder he was fit.

Tree roots clawed their way across the earthy ground and reminded her of illustrations she'd seen in books depicting hidden routes to secret worlds.

Careful not to trip, she continued on until she reached the top where she saw Josh's mansion and the expanse of his beautiful garden.

She stopped under the fringed canopy of greenery that arched over the end of the pathway. Even if Josh had been home he probably wouldn't have seen her peering out at him. She'd no intention of intruding. Josh was a handsome mistake. One she planned to learn from rather than repeat.

After lingering for a moment, she headed back down to the shore.

Abby wasn't sure if the muscles in her thighs ached more on the way up or the way down the pathway. Probably both. At the bottom she stepped out into the bright sunlight again and walked further along the shore road to the far end of the bay. On the way back she decided to go down on to the sand. The tide was out and the sand was fairly dry.

It had been a while since she'd walked along any sandy shore. Living in the city had kept her life more contained than she'd realised. The sense of freedom here was wonderful.

She planned to come back down later, kitted out for an afternoon down the shore. There was a folding chair in the shed she could use to sit on and sew her favourite hexies. Fussy cutting pieces of fabric from prints with flowers, butterflies, bees and other sweet items were often included in her quilts, and basting the hexagon fabric shapes was one of the joys of sewing. Give her a load of hexies to stitch and a cup of tea and she'd soon relax. It was a great way to unwind after work, and she could stitch them while watching television. Her hexie quilts were a pleasure to create and she loved mixing different fabrics prints together to make a finished design.

Breathing in more fresh sea air, she headed back to the cottage.

Her sewing machine was set up in the lounge, but she'd still to unpack all of her fabric stash and create an area for her quilt work. There was a traditional dresser that had handy shelves and cupboard space to store her tidy boxes of sewing accessories, and she packed everything away before tackling her fabric stash.

Before beginning to fold each piece so she could easily see the selection available, she opened the patio doors to allow the warm air from the garden to waft in. It was the greatest feeling to have a lovely garden like this, and it made it seem like the lounge extended out into the sunlight. This helped her see the true colours of the fabrics. She sorted them by hue or type of print. She also collected precious tiny scraps that were so useful for making her quilts. The larger pieces, such as fat quarters, were folded and stacked on the shelves, and small pieces were stored in boxes and pretty containers. The colourful array of the fabrics when she'd finished tidying and arranging them looked so pretty, and she felt the urge to start sewing.

However, with lunchtime approaching, she went through to the kitchen and prepared a tasty lunch. She scrubbed the Ayrshire tatties and put them on to boil. In a separate pot she boiled up the fresh carrots, cabbage and onion.

While these cooked, she washed and chopped the greentails, and cut a slice of bread from the crusty loaf she'd bought from Minnie's shop.

When the tatties were ready, she put them on a plate, topped with a knob of butter, sprinkled with greentails and a dash of black pepper. She served up the medley of vegetables and added a pinch of sea salt and a spoonful of salad cream.

She then sat down at the kitchen table and enjoyed her lunch. Yes, she was alone, but she didn't feel lonely. She'd made her heart vulnerable with her feelings for Josh and been swiped down. Sometimes life just didn't give her the breaks when it came to romance, but she was determined not to let it spoil the new life she had here in this lovely cottage.

115

With the seashore right on her doorstep she didn't plan on moping around. Sunny days like this were made for spending on the shore. And whatever the weather, quilting always made her feel better.

Josh's knuckles ached as he signed the documents authorising a transfer of funds from his bank account to Keera's firm. He wanted everything in writing, triple checked, sealed and sorted.

He'd woken up before the dawn. Unable to get back to sleep for uneasy thoughts of how he'd upset Abby, he'd decided to take his energy and wrath out on the punching bag in the hotel's luxury gym. It hung there looking new, a token gesture that few had used. Ignoring the racks of gleaming weights and other equipment, he'd set about the bag, almost punching it off the chain it dangled from.

He hadn't brought his gloves or training mitts with him, so he fought raw, feeling his knuckles connect with the bag.

He barely broke a sweat. Maybe he was fitter than he thought. Or perhaps his body was pumped with so much adrenalin from the rage of his own stupidity that his system had gone into overdrive to cope with the intensity of his feelings. Thoughts of Abby burned through him. He'd never felt like this about any woman, and never expected it to hit him so strong and so sudden. He sensed he could be happy with her, content, and they'd build a life together and hopefully raise a family. Something he longed for.

Pounding the bag on his own, having the entire gym to himself, he'd let rip with every punch, jab, upper cut and right hook he had in his armoury until his knuckles felt fist to burst. They didn't of course because he knew how to throw a punch without causing any damage. That didn't mean his knuckles didn't hurt as much as his heart. But neither showed it.

'Something wrong, Josh?' Keera's words jarred him from his thoughts.

He pushed the paperwork across Keera's desk for her to sign.

'Sign and date them,' he said. 'I want everything legal.'

Keera pursed her lips, emphasising her deep red lipstick. She was wearing a figure enhancing skirt suit in a similar tone. If she was trying to send a signal to him that she was vibrant and available, she'd missed her target. All Josh wanted was to finish the work and head back home. Almost done now.

116

Abby carried the little folding chair down on to the sand. The shore wall rose high above her, shielding her from the breeze, creating a warm backdrop where she settled down to enjoy an afternoon sewing hexies outdoors and enjoying the sea air.

A few people were dotted along the shoreline. No one broached on anyone else's space, and she liked that the locals understood the benefit of giving each other a welcoming nod while allowing each other to relax on their own.

The village wasn't a tourist trap. From what Minnie had told her, there were other towns along the coast that catered for that. This left the village with a life of its own which suited the easy pace of the villagers. They preferred to enjoy the summer amid their own community without being overcrowded by holidaymakers. Visitors were always made welcome, but life here didn't change and become busy in the summer months or holiday seasons, and this was something that Abby appreciated too.

With a lap size quilt on her chair for comfort, she kicked her pumps off and felt the warm sand beneath her feet as she prepared to stitch the hexies. These were easy to sew on the go, and she used to take them with her to the ad agency to make during lunchtimes when she wasn't working at her desk and grabbing a sandwich while continuing to deal with clients.

Her sewing bag contained all she needed — small pieces of hexagon shaped cotton fabric that she'd pre–cut, paper templates, scissors, pins, needle and thread. The paper pieces were slightly smaller than the fabric to allow her to fold the fabric over the paper and baste each hexie with a few stitches. The stitches and the papers would be removed later when she started to sew the hexies together to create a quilt.

She began sewing and relaxing in the heat of the sun. Sheer bliss.

A few people were in swimming, and she was tempted to join them, but unsure of the temperature, she put her quilting down after an hour's sewing, rolled up the hems of her jeans and left her things on her chair while she ventured in for a paddle.

The water was warmer than she'd imagined and if it hadn't been so late now in the afternoon, with the sun becoming a burnished gold as the intensity of it mellowed, she might have run up to the cottage, grabbed her swimsuit and gone for a swim. But there was always tomorrow. There was definitely a break in the stormy weather and it felt like summer had arrived.

Abby prepared an easy dinner, eager to sit at her sewing machine and finish one of the quilts she planned to sell. The quilting bee website launched the following night when the members met up again for their regular bee evening at the tea shop, and she wanted to have her own website ready too. Some of the quilts she'd been sewing only needed minor tasks completed, such as stitching the binding or a bit of machine quilting to finish the design. And she had a stash of quilts she'd made.

She sliced the leftover Ayrshire tatties she'd cooked and served them with a crisp green salad drizzled with herb dressing.

She also dug out her turquoise swimsuit and hung it up on the wardrobe door as a reminder that she intending going swimming.

In the early evening Abby baked a batch of shortbread and fruit cakes. She was starting to get into a routine and hoped this would save time in the morning. The aroma of the rich fruit cakes made with sultanas, raisins, fruit peel and glacé cherries filled the kitchen and wafted through to the lounge.

While leafing through Netta's recipe books and files, she noticed that the covers were well–worn from years of use. She didn't want to replace the covers because they were part of the original books, so instead she made quilted covers that slipped on over the top.

She used scraps of pretty print fabric in shades of pink, blue and yellow, ditsy floral prints with roses, bluebells and primroses, and ran them up in her sewing machine, adding ribbon trims. When finished and on the books and files, they looked so lovely displayed on the kitchen shelf.

There was no storm this evening. The night was calm and it was only when it was time to go to bed that Abby closed the patio doors.

She climbed into bed and gazed out at the silvery sea. Her swimsuit hanging on the wardrobe reminded her that she was going swimming tomorrow.

She tugged her quilt up and wondered if the two quilts she'd made that Josh had bought were still in his mansion and on his bed. Her thoughts then drifted to him spending another night away with his ex, and no word from him.

She wished she hadn't sold her quilts to him. They didn't belong there in his mansion or on his bed and neither did she.

Fluffing her pillows, she scolded herself for thinking of things that made her upset, and went to sleep.

CHAPTER ELEVEN

Gordon was surprised to see Abby swimming towards him during his early morning dip in the sea.

'I'm impressed,' he called to her.

'So am I,' she said. When she'd cast off her clothes and tucked them in the basket of her bike after making her cake deliveries, she felt slightly exposed in her turquoise swimsuit. Cut high on the thighs, it was a figure flattering design. 'The water's a bit cold. I think I'm more of an afternoon swimmer when the sea has had time to warm up.'

'The sea's always warmer here midday and afternoon,' Gordon agreed. 'But I can offer you a hot breakfast.'

'I don't want to keep imposing on you,' she said.

'You're not, besides, you've been so helpful advising me on selling my confectionery on my website. Let me glean some more information from you while I ply you with a tasty cooked breakfast.'

'Okay, it's a deal.'

They swam together for a few more minutes before racing each other along the sand and up to the tea shop.

Abby jumped up and down. 'I win!' She'd parked her bike outside his tea shop and packed a towel in her basket. She grabbed it and began to dry herself.

Gordon flicked his towel around his neck and conceded. 'You're a fast runner. Maybe not as fast as Josh, but I think he'd have to up his game to beat you.' He paused, realising he'd brought up Josh. 'Sorry, I didn't mean to—'

Abby cut–in. 'It's okay.'

They went inside and made no more mention of Josh, but Gordon knew she was still upset and clearly had feelings for him.

'I'll be down in a moment,' he said, running up the stairs.

'Okay, I'll get changed at the back of the shop,' she replied.

While Gordon jumped in the shower upstairs, Abby slipped out of her wet suit and into her jeans and top. She towel dried her hair, tied it back in a ponytail and put her damp towel and swimsuit in a bag outside on her bike.

She'd just gone into the kitchen when Gordon hurried in, dressed and ready for work.

He opened up his laptop and accessed his website. 'Any advice would be welcome.'

Abby created a file and noted down several things he could do to improve the look of the website while Gordon cooked their breakfast.

'If you want, I'll write some descriptions for you to help sell your confectionery and email it to you later,' she offered.

'That would be great,' he said, buttering the toast and sharing the scrambled eggs between the two of them.

Over breakfast she advised him on various aspects of his tea shop business advertising.

By the time she left, he was buzzing with ideas.

Abby showered at home, rinsed her swimsuit and hung it up to dry, and then started working on her quilts.

'Aren't you coming into my office today?' Keera asked, phoning Josh at his hotel room.

'No, I've finished everything online. I don't need to come in. We're done.' His voice sounded deep and determined.

He heard her sigh. 'So that's it then?'

'Yes. I've recommended a couple of financial managers. Their contact numbers are in the file I've emailed to you. They have a reliable reputation. Hire one of them to sort out your business. Good luck with it.'

There was an awkward pause before Keera said, 'Thanks for your help, Josh.' She paused again before their last goodbye. 'In my own way, I really did love you.'

For the first time in a long while he believed what she said to him, but it changed nothing.

'Goodbye, Keera.'

And he was gone.

Josh drove away from the city in his sleek dark car, merging with the busy traffic. The drive to the coast seemed to take forever because he just wanted to be home again, and to try and mend things with Abby.

The sun cast a bronze glow over the landscape as he finally reached the coast. A glimpse through the trees showed the water shining like liquid amber. The mellow pace made him slow down and head along to his mansion.

He parked in the driveway and carried his overnight bag, laptop and briefcase inside. He put his things down in the study then ran upstairs and jumped in the shower, wanting to wash the remainder of an awkward time away to feel okay again.

Emerging clean and fresh, he dressed in smart casuals, trousers and a shirt in classy, neutral tones, and then headed down the pathway to the shore. He didn't run. He wasn't out for a run, though the temptation to hurry to Abby's cottage was strong. He hoped she'd be in.

He knocked on the door and received no answer. Peering through the living room window he saw that she wasn't at home.

Then it dawned on him. This was a quilting bee night. She'd be at the tea shop. Bad timing.

Abby had just arrived at the tea shop. Gordon had baked a celebration cake topped with vanilla frosting and sprinkles for the ladies launch night. There was a party atmosphere, and although they were only pressing the button to make their website live, it had become a night of cheers and very little sewing.

The ladies grouped together for a photograph, and were about to launch the website on Abby's laptop that was set up at the back of the tea shop. Everyone was buzzing with excitement.

'I have something special,' said Gordon, hurrying through to the front of the tea shop where a few customers were having tea and cakes. He'd stashed a large bottle of champagne behind the counter and grabbed it to take it through to pop the cork as they pressed the button.

That's when he saw the brooding figure of Josh peering in the tea shop window.

Josh had plucked up the nerve to come in and face Abby and the ladies, but Gordon barred him from entering.

'Not tonight, Josh,' Gordon said firmly, clutching the bottle of champagne in one hand and barring him with the other hand. He managed to get Josh to step outside where they could talk without the bee members seeing them.

'I want to talk to Abby,' said Josh.

'No, not now. The ladies are having a party to launch their new website. They're about to press the button, and you're not coming in to spoil things.' The forcefulness of Gordon's tone was clear.

A tense standoff burned between the two men for a moment before Gordon spoke.

'I'm not looking to fight with you, Josh.'

'I didn't think you were, Gordon.'

Calmly, Josh nodded and walked away.

Judy came scurrying towards Gordon. 'Is something wrong? We're about to press the button.'

'Josh is back,' he confided. 'I wouldn't let him in. I didn't want him upsetting your evening. Don't tell the others.'

Judy zipped her lips, and then they both pasted on happy smiles and went through to the others.

Gordon held up the bottle of champagne as if this was what had kept him.

'Oh, bubbly!' Minnie exclaimed.

The ladies huddled around Abby's laptop. She hovered her finger over the key that would unlock the website from being private to public. Several hands reached over, so they could all be part of the launch moment.

'Are we ready to launch the website?' Abby asked, smiling at them.

'Yes,' came the unanimous reply.

With a flourish, they all pressed down on Abby's hand as she hit the button. The screen showed the website was now available online.

'We have lift–off!' Minnie announced.

The ladies cheered.

Gordon opened the champagne and poured it into their glasses.

Judy tipped her glass against Abby's and made an announcement. 'Cheers to you, Abby, for encouraging us to have our own website. We're proud to have you as a member of our quilting bee.'

More cheers, applause and laughter filled the tea shop, and Gordon took photos of the ladies all together drinking champagne and enjoying their celebration cake.

The evening continued with chatter, sewing, checking the website and more champagne, tea and cake.

Josh walked back along the shore and then up the pathway to his house. Gordon had been right not to let him into the tea shop. It would've spoiled the ladies special evening.

The shadows of the trees in the evening light added to the heavy feeling weighing down on him. Disappointment made the walk up the pathway a chore. Dashed hopes were always more tiring than any workout.

Arriving home he headed upstairs to his bedroom, striped off and changed into a pair of boxer shorts. He stood outside on the balcony breathing in the sea air, glad to be back from the city. It was a balmy night and would've been perfect for walking along the shore with Abby, explaining what he'd done, assuring her that Keera wasn't part of his life now, and apologising for causing the mess he was in.

The muscles in his broad back tensed as he leaned his hands on the balcony, wringing out his frustration on the balustrade. Far in the distance the lights of the tea shop and bar restaurant cast a welcoming glow on the shore road. No welcome for him though. Not tonight.

Pushing back from the balcony, he went inside, flicked the lights off and lay on top of his bed. The nightglow shone in from the balcony as he thought things through. Tomorrow he'd start afresh and find the right moment to talk to Abby. What he needed was an undisturbed night's sleep, something he'd missed since he'd left for the city.

The air coming in from the balcony was mild, and he'd lived here long enough to sense that hot weather was on its way. The recent thunderstorms often signalled the approach of a warm spell.

As he lay there, he realised he was lying on Abby's quilt. He ran his hands over the surface of the fabric, taking comfort from knowing this was something she'd made. It was a beautiful quilt, sewn by a beautiful woman.

He sighed heavily. He was lucky to have to have someone as kind and warm–hearted in his life. He might be on the edges of her life right now, but he planned to remedy the trouble he'd gotten himself into. Abby was worth fighting for, and for all the fights he'd had in the ring, this one meant more to him than any of them.

'So, are you up for a swim again tomorrow morning?' Gordon asked chirpily as Abby and the ladies got ready to leave the tea shop. They'd all enjoyed the party.

Abby wasn't sure. 'I don't know...'

'Come on,' he encouraged her. 'One more morning.' He glanced outside the window at the night sky filled with stars above the calm sea. 'It could be a scorcher tomorrow.'

There was the sense of a heatwave, and as Scotland's weather was unpredictable, she thought she'd better make the most of it.

'Okay,' Abby agreed. 'And I've emailed some extra ideas for the confectionery on your website,' she remembered to tell him. 'Check your email. We'll chat in the morning, when I beat you again.'

Minnie was intrigued. 'What did Abby beat you at Gordon?'

'Everything,' Gordon joked. 'Including running. Abby is fast.'

'You'll have to up your game, Gordon,' Judy said, giving him a knowing look. She knew Gordon had feelings for Abby, but now that Josh was back on the scene, Gordon would need to gear up or keep his feelings to himself.

'I'm doing my best, Judy,' Gordon replied.

Judy made sure that Abby was the first to leave. Gordon and the ladies waved her off.

The moment Abby was out of earshot, Judy and Gordon explained what had happened earlier.

Pearl blinked. 'Josh is back?'

'He is,' Gordon told her. 'So there's either going to be fireworks or a damp squib showdown. Josh obviously wants to talk to her.'

'Should we warn her?' Minnie asked.

'I'm going to tell her tomorrow morning,' Gordon explained. 'I didn't want to ruin her night, or give her an uneasy sleep.'

The women nodded that he'd done the right thing.

As she walked back to her cottage from the tea shop, Abby glanced up in the direction of Josh's mansion. There were no lights on to gauge exactly where it was, but she'd a rough idea that it was behind a particular area of trees. He obviously wasn't back yet, and was enjoying another night away doing whatever he was up to with his ex.

Not that she cared, she lied to herself.

Back home, she unpacked her laptop, checked that the new website was still working, and got ready for bed. She planned to launch her website tomorrow, having decided not to clash with the bee members launch.

She'd prepared emails ready to send to potential customers to help get the sales going on the quilting bee website. From years of working in the ad agency, whenever she had an idea or a task that needed done, she'd do it rather than let things pile up. So, she'd written an email that mentioned the quilting bee products were now available.

She was pleased with the website. The prices were fair but competitive, the quilts were all original hand sewn products of high quality, the photos displayed their beauty, and the editorial descriptions were an accurate depiction of each quilt. Great products, well–presented, excellent prices with discounts for bulk buys and the ability to order custom made quilts. Post and packaging was included and fast delivery was provided.

This type of work was second nature to her, so she sent the emails and hoped that some orders would come from them. The ladies also aimed to start getting the word out on social media that their quilts were for sale. Abby planned to follow up with other ways to advertise to specific target markets, but closed the laptop for now and went to bed.

The early morning sunlight shone off the surface of the sea and the air already had some heat in it.

Abby made the cake deliveries as before, and then headed down to the shore in her swimsuit, leaving her bicycle and clothes at Gordon's tea shop.

Gordon was there in his red trunks, waiting for her, and had just finished blowing up a beach ball. He threw it up into the air, caught it, and gave Abby a challenging look.

Abby shook her head. 'You've got to be kidding me.'

'Nope. Though you'll probably beat me.'

'Do I even want to?'

Gordon laughed and then looked guilty.

'Something wrong?' she asked him.

He nodded. 'I found out something last night and didn't tell you.'

She sensed what was wrong before he told her.

'Josh is back,' he said. 'He came to the tea shop last night to talk to you, but I wouldn't let him in. I didn't want him ruining the quilting bee website launch party.'

He waited for her reaction.

'Thank you, Gordon,' she said clearly.

He stopped holding his breath. 'You're not upset with me?'

'Not at all. I wouldn't have wanted the party spoiled either. Do any of the women know?'

'Judy knew, but we kept it a secret from the others until the end of the night. We waited until you'd gone before discussing things.'

'You made the right decision,' she said.

'So, what are you going to do now?' he asked.

'Go for a swim — after I beat you at your beach ball challenge.'

Gordon laughed, relieved that she wasn't going to dwell on Josh. He hit the ball high into the air for her to catch.

Abby caught it, making it look easy.

'This is not going to go well for me, is it?' he said, joking with her.

'No, Gordon, I don't think it is.'

With it being so early in the morning, they thought they had the shore to themselves and that no one would hear their laughter as they played catch on the sand and splashed around in the water.

Josh had slept remarkably well for a man with a lot on his mind.

He knew Abby would be busy with her baking in the morning, so he planned to talk to her around lunchtime.

He wanted to go for a run down the shore, but didn't want to risk encountering Abby when she was cycling along the road. He needed to talk to her properly and in private. So he put on his blue swimming trunks under his light training gear and ran down the pathway to the shore for a swim. Abby wouldn't notice him swimming and he needed to work off some excess energy.

The shore looked empty and he thought he had it all to himself, but as he swam along he heard laughter and screams of joy. Some folks were up as early as him and in the mood for high jinks.

It was only as he swam nearer that he saw it was Abby and Gordon, playing with a beach ball. Her squeals of happy laughter tore through him, and he paused, treading water, watching what happened next...

'No, Gordon, no!' Abby squealed as Gordon lifted her up in his arms and ran over to throw her in the sea.

'Concede the point, Abby. You cheated with that last throw.'

'I didn't cheat. You throw like a girl.'

Gordon roared with laughter and then threatened to throw her into the water. 'Did you say I should throw a girl?'

Abby clung to him, wrapping her arms tight around his neck and shoulders, not prepared to let go.

'If you throw me, Gordon, I'm taking you with me.'

Struggling, play wrestling, fooling around and breathless laughing, they tumbled into the water anyway and emerged splashing a giggling like a couple of kids.

Josh's heart and hopes sank to the depths of the sea. He'd feared if he stepped back, Gordon or Euan would make a move on Abby. Seems like Gordon did, and Abby was clearly happy with him.

He dived under the water and swam back along, heading in the direction of home. Underwater he couldn't hear how happy she was with Gordon, only the roar of the sea water as he powered away, occasionally coming up for air.

Now far enough away to wade out without them seeing him, he strode up the sand to where he'd left his clothes and shoes. Slipping on his shoes, he grabbed his clothes and ran up the pathway. No one saw him. Running up the path soaking wet was becoming a habit he thought, remembering the night it rained.

He stood in the shower at home and let the water wash over him. Having seen Abby and Gordon together, he changed his mind about talking to Abby. No wonder Gordon had challenged him at the tea shop, barring him from coming in. It made sense now. They'd become a couple, or were at least heading that way.

Gordon and Abby finally walked back up to the tea shop, too exhausted to race each other this time.

'I won,' she said, making claim to winning their antics whether or not it was true.

'Fine, okay, I got beaten by a girl again,' he conceded happily.

They went inside and fell into their previous routine.

'Breakfast?' he asked her.

'Yes, I'll start making the tea.'

Over their tea and toast they discussed Gordon's website.

'I read your email,' he said. 'Great ideas. I'll take photos of the chocolates and confectionery. I'm a lucky man to have your input.'

'You are very welcome,' she said.

He leaned forward and for a moment became serious.

'Listen,' he said, 'I know you like Josh and he likes you. Despite all that's happened I still think there's a high chance you're going to get together. If you end up dating Josh as his girlfriend, promise me I won't lose you as a friend.'

'I promise, but I'm not to sure that I'll get together with Josh.'

'Oh, I think you will.'

The conversation went back to advice on selling his confectionery, and while Abby used his laptop to give him notes, he started to prepare the fresh cream cakes for the tea shop.

When Abby got back to the cottage a letter had been dropped through her door.

She opened it and read the message. It was from Euan, telling her that the marquee was going to be erected in his field the following weekend for the ceilidh. He assured her that the work would be done in a day, and no one would trespass in her cottage garden.

She'd almost forgotten about the ceilidh, the first of many that were planned. Euan was the next to host the ceilidh in his field. At least the dancing was right on her doorstep, and it was only for one night that weekend. She was quite looking forward to it.

Abby was sewing one of her quilts when her phone rang. It was Judy.

'Are you busy?' Judy sounded excited.

'I'm finishing one of my quilts.' She hoped to have it finished by lunchtime.

'Have you launched your website yet?'

'Yes, I launched it about an hour ago.' Abby had a cup of tea and a fairy cake with sprinkles to celebrate. 'Has something happened?'

'Oh, yes. You know the emails you sent out to advertise the quilting bee website?'

'Yes.'

'Well, we've had a response on our online contact form from one of the boutique hotels. The owner asked if he could phone to discuss placing an order, so I gave him my number and I'm just off the phone chatting to him.'

'What did he say?'

'He's redecorating his boutique hotel in an upmarket part of the city. There are over twenty rooms, many with twin beds, and he wants a different quilt for each bed. He's selected the quilts he likes, but asked if we have any with bees and butterflies, and I thought of your quilts. He wants to arrange a courier to pick them all up in one delivery. He needs a fast delivery and will arrange this for tomorrow if he can see the other quilts.'

'My quilts?'

'Yes, so can you help me deal with this?' said Judy.

'I'm on my way.'

Abby grabbed her laptop, jumped on her bike and cycled like the wind up to the bar restaurant.

She was aware of Gordon watering his hanging flower baskets outside the tea shop as she whizzed by shouting, 'I'll explain everything later. We've sold quilts.'

Gordon blinked, got the gist of the message and watched her jump off her bike and dash in to see Judy.

Judy whisked her through to the small office adjoining the bar.

Jock gave Abby the thumbs up as he continued to serve drinks to customers.

Judy closed the office door and they sat down with their laptops.

'Let's not mess this up,' said Judy.

'We won't. I have photos of my bee and butterfly quilts here. We can email the pictures to him right now. I've got the descriptions too.'

Within minutes they'd composed an email, attached photos of Abby's two quilts, added a couple of extra for choice — a dragonfly design and one with seahorses, and sent it off to the man for approval.

And then they waited.

Judy flopped back in her chair. 'Wow! Just wow!'

Abby smiled. 'I know, it's great. But now you'll all have to sew more quilts to restock the website.'

'Ah, but most of us have a stack of quilts. We put a few up for sale, but we've got more folded on shelves and tucked away that we can use. That'll give us a buffer so we can sew more.'

'That's handy,' said Abby. 'I've advertised the majority of mine for sale on my website, but I'm working on new designs.'

Jock knocked on the door and peeked in. 'Tea, cocktails or a shot of whisky?'

Judy nodded at him. 'Yes.'

Jock laughed and left them to get on with things.

'Do you have all of these quilts finished?' Judy asked her, looking at the pictures.

'Yes, and I can have them all checked and folded ready by teatime,' Abby assured her.

'Perfect,' Judy said smiling.

'Does Minnie, Pearl or any of the other members know?'

'Nooo, I want to secure the sale before getting their hopes up.'

'What other quilts did he like?'

Judy pointed to the selection he'd made. 'He's obviously looking for different styles so thankfully we've all got at least one quilt sold — if he confirms the order.'

Ping!

Judy checked the email. 'Order confirmed.' She read the details and laughed. 'He's bought the dragonfly and seahorse quilts too.'

As they were laughing, Jock knocked and handed in a tray with tea and drinks.

Judy was beaming and gave him an excited hug. 'We've sold our quilts. Lots of them. The order is paid for and a courier is picking them up tomorrow morning.'

Jock gave them a cheer. 'That's great!' Then he left them to it.

Judy picked up her phone. 'I'm calling an emergency quilting bee meeting here tonight. The members will have to bring their quilts so I can get them packed ready for delivery.'

Abby was glad she was there to hear the squeals of excitement as each member was told they'd made a sale or two. Minnie's reaction was particularly vocal. Abby drank her tea while Judy finished by making a call to Pearl.

'I don't usually phone Pearl when she's at work,' said Judy, 'but this is a quilting emergency.'

Pearl was in the mansion kitchen checking the store cupboards were well stocked when Judy phoned her.

'Pearl? It's me, Judy. You've sold two quilts. We've all sold at least one quilt to a single buyer. He owns a boutique hotel. I'm calling an emergency quilting bee meeting tonight at the bar restaurant.'

'I've sold two quilts?' Pearl sounded delighted.

'Bring them with you tonight. The burgundy one and the one with the wee birds and bluebells. They're all being picked up by courier tomorrow morning.'

'I'll be there. Thanks, Judy.'

'Have you seen Josh?' Judy asked quickly.

'A glimpse,' Pearl told her. 'He's been working in his study all morning. Doesn't seem happy.'

'Okay, I'll tell Abby.'

'See you later,' said Pearl before hanging up.

When Pearl finished her call with Judy she was bursting with excitement. She checked the time. She was due to finish work in a few minutes having started early in the morning. Picking up her bag, she walked through to the hall to leave. Then she decided to knock on the study door.

'Yes?' Josh called through.

Pearl opened the door slightly. 'I've sold two quilts. We've all sold quilts. The quilting bee website is a success. Okay, I'm away now.' She closed the door and hurried out, eager to get back home to sort out her quilts.

Josh ran after her. 'Wait.' He caught up with her outside. 'You've sold quilts?'

Pearl paused. 'Yes, Judy phoned me. We're having a meeting tonight to get them ready for delivery.'

Josh frowned. 'That was fast work. I thought you launched the website last night.'

'We did, but Abby used her advertising expertise and sent emails to potential customers and one of them has bought our quilts,' Pearl summarised.

'Good on Abby,' he said, sensing Pearl wanted to get on.

'Yes, she's great.'

As Pearl walked away Josh stood there nodding. Abby was great. The disappointment hit him again. Gordon was a lucky man.

Abby cycled quickly back along the shore road to her cottage, leaving Judy to finish the cocktails.

She wanted to carefully fold and wrap the quilts she'd sold.

Although she was happy for herself, she was more delighted for the ladies. All their work was worthwhile. She didn't think this type of bulk sale would be a regular occurrence, but it was a nice boost for everyone.

The quilting bee was buzzing in the bar restaurant function room. All the members were there with their quilts.

Judy took charge of the itinerary, making sure the order was correct and all quilts accounted for. She was good at this.

The evening was so hot that iced tea was served up rather than their usual cuppas. Abby drank half of the contents of her glass, relishing the cool, refreshing drink, before realising it was potent.

'I thought this was iced tea,' Abby said to Judy.

Judy smiled. 'There's tea in it.'

Pearl laughed.

Minnie fanned herself with a quilt pattern from her bag. 'It's potent stuff, Judy. I'm discombobulated enough with the quilt sales and Shawn.'

'Tell Abby about Shawn coming into your shop this morning,' Judy encouraged Minnie.

Abby nodded, wanting to hear about it.

'Shawn came in with his fresh eggs delivery and wanted to make sure I was going with him as his date to the ceilidh,' Minnie explained. 'He says he's wearing his kilt and has something special for me in his sporran. I don't know whether to be flattered or run for the hills.' She fanned herself again.

Abby and the other women laughed.

'Oh, you can laugh, but I don't know what he thinks he's going to get from me except a whirl around the dance floor.' Then Minnie shifted the focus to Abby. 'Any update on you and Josh?'

'Nothing,' said Abby. 'I haven't heard from him.'

Minnie frowned. 'I thought he wanted to talk to you?'

'I guess he changed his mind,' Abby replied.

'I'll see what I can find out,' Pearl promised.

Judy folded the last of the quilts. 'Remember, if any of you need a dress for the ceilidh, you're welcome to borrow one from my wardrobes. I've got some pretty tartan dresses. I was going through a plaid phase last year and bought and made a few nice wee numbers.'

'Have you still got that swirly tartan skirt I borrowed before?' Minnie asked. 'It was lovely for the dancing.'

'Yes, pop upstairs and help yourself,' said Judy.

Minnie got up. 'Thanks, Judy. I thought I'd wear it with my white blouse and a tartan sash.' Minnie headed upstairs to get the skirt.

'Are you sure you don't need a ceilidh dress, Abby?' Judy asked.

'No, I've got a couple of dresses that'll do. I might even wear the other tea dress you gave me, and I have a tartan sash I wore to a Hogmanay party.'

'If you change your mind, let me know,' said Judy.

With her head buzzing with excitement about the quilting bee sales, and from the potent iced tea, Abby walked back to her cottage.

It was such a beautiful night. She gazed over at the calm sea and breathed in the evening air. The sky arched in gradients of midnight blues along the length of the bay.

Glancing up at the hillside, she saw the lights were on in Josh's mansion. An unexpected sense of longing tore through her, taking her aback at the strength of her feelings when she thought about how close he was and yet so far out of reach. If she'd had the confidence she'd have marched up there right now and asked him why he didn't want to talk to her when he'd said he did. They'd argue, but maybe they could settle their differences, and she'd give him the benefit of the doubt that Judy had advised her to do.

But she didn't have the confidence, not tonight, so she sighed and continued walking to her cottage.

She was so deep in thought that she didn't see Josh standing further along the shore road, near the entrance to the pathway. He was out for a late night run, and due to the heat he was wearing lightweight black training trousers and a black vest, boxer style.

He was watching her, longing to run up to her, wrap her in his arms and promise never to do anything so foolish again to risk losing her. And he might have done, but she looked so happy, as if bubbling with excitement. He knew it wasn't a quilting bee night, and seeing the direction she'd walked from, he assumed she'd had a nice evening at the tea shop with Gordon.

Pushing aside the urge to take a chance and fight for her, he watched her go inside the cottage, and then he ran down on to the shore, pounding along the sand, a lone figure racing faster and faster, a silhouette against the vast sea.

CHAPTER TWELVE

The courier arrived just before midday to pick up the quilts. Abby was there to help Judy.

As the van drove away, Minnie came hurrying along with Bracken bounding beside her.

'I saw the van arrive,' Minnie gasped. 'Is that the order away?'

'It is,' Judy assured her, giving Bracken a welcoming pat.

'I can't leave my shop for long,' said Minnie, 'but I wanted the benefit of seeing our quilts on their way.'

Bracken bounded around Abby and she bent down to give him a hug.

'We'll start taking more photos and get those uploaded on to the website,' said Judy, taking charge of getting things organised.

Abby glanced up at the blue sky. 'It's going to be another scorcher. I think I'll do some sewing again down the shore.'

Bracken's ears perked up.

'I have to get back to my shop,' said Minnie, seeing a couple of customers heading inside. 'Come on, Bracken.'

The dog hesitated, but then came to heel beside Minnie.

'Do you want me to take him for a W.A.L.K. along the shore?' Abby offered.

Bracken barked in the affirmative.

'He knows the phrase,' said Minnie, laughing. 'But if you would take him for a quick jaunt, he'd love it.' She handed Abby the dog's lead that was in her apron pocket and his play ball. 'He enjoys a wee game of fetch.'

Abby wasn't sure which one of them was more tuckered out from running around on the shore, chasing the ball and playing fetch.

Giggling and breathless, she sat down on the sand, leaned her back against the shore wall, and relaxed for a few minutes. Bracken flopped beside her.

It was then that she saw a man running along the edge of the sea. She cupped her hand to shield her eyes from the dazzling sunlight. Yes, it was Josh. Her heart squeezed and a sense of longing charged through her. He hadn't seen her, not yet, but he was heading in her direction. If he saw her, would he come over?

Every part of his physique was honed, and he looked like a fit fighter. But would he fight for her, for them to be together? She didn't want to be so affected when she noticed the strong muscles in his arms, the cut of his broad shoulders and long, lean thighs. He looked so handsome but serious, as if his thoughts weighed heavily on him.

Any second now he would surely see her. Her heart rate quickened, increasing with the pace of his strides as he ran closer. Would he look over at her...?

'Did you get my note?' a deep voice sounded down on her over the sea wall.

Abby looked up and saw Euan.

'Yes, thanks for letting me know about the marquee for the ceilidh,' she said, almost as an aside as she kept looking at Josh.

Euan saw where her attention lay. 'Has he made up with you yet?'

'No.'

'More fool him,' Euan remarked and then walked away.

By now Josh had run past. Had he seen her? She didn't know.

She watched him run away along the coast, feeling a dagger of hurt through her heart.

As if sensing her upset, the dog sat up and offered her a comforting paw.

She stood up and brushed the sand from her clothes. 'Come on, Bracken, let's get you back to the shop for a drink of water.'

She walked him along the grassy verge to get the sand off his paws. He had more energy left than she had and bounded along beside her all the way back.

Josh ran home, taking a different route, rather than have his heart skewered again seeing Abby.

He'd just got a glimpse of her when Euan appeared. Bad timing again.

If Euan hadn't been chatting to her, he would've gone over and talked to her.

Bracken padded into the grocery shop with his tail wagging.

'He's still got some sand on his paws,' Abby told Minnie.

'Awe, that's fine. He seems happy.' Minnie made a fuss of him, and brought his water bowl through as he sat in his basket.

'Help yourself to a cold drink from the fridge,' Minnie said to Abby. 'I think Bracken's tuckered you out.'

Abby explained why she looked a bit deflated, not just from running around with the dog.

'You saw Josh?' said Minnie.

Abby explained what happened.

'That was awkward timing with Euan,' Minnie agreed.

'I don't know if Josh saw me, but he ran on.' Abby sounded disappointed.

'I'm about to close the shop for half an hour for lunch. Would you like to join me? It's just a bowl of soup and salad.'

'Yes, thanks Minnie.'

Abby helped make the tea and cut the bread in the shop's small kitchen while Minnie heated the soup and prepared the salad.

Over lunch they chatted about men, love and romance, and how to put the world to rights.

During the next few days, Abby was busy in the mornings baking cakes, and in the afternoons she stitched her quilts outdoors, either down the shore or in her back garden sitting under the apple tree.

She'd had a couple of sales of her quilts on her website, and further interest shown from an interior designer.

Gordon had taken new photos of his confectionery, and Abby had written the editorials for him, describing how delicious they were. She'd advised him to create a brand logo for his packaging, and to rename each piece of confectionery with an enticing name that helped describe the taste or ingredients. So Gordon was happy. Some mornings she went swimming with him, and other days she swam in the afternoon, taking a break from her quilting to enjoy the lovely weather while it lasted.

She felt the fittest she'd been in years, but she still couldn't forget about Josh.

With the quilting bee held two evenings a week, the days rolled around quickly to their next meeting at the tea shop.

Buying fabric to make their new quilts was the hot topic being discussed when Abby arrived to join the ladies at the bee.

Gordon was busy serving his regular customers in the front shop. Abby waved to him and went through to the function room at the back where the whirring of sewing machines merged with the excited chatter.

Abby sat down in the midst of the happy melee. 'Sorry I'm a bit late, but I was on the phone to a potential customer. I have news.'

Judy was bursting to tell her something. 'We've got news too. Lots of news.'

'You go first,' Minnie encouraged Abby.

'An interior designer contacted me. He's interested in buying two of my quilts — one with the thistle fabric and one with the heather print.'

'Those are lovely quilts, Abby,' Minnie enthused.

Judy nodded. 'They are.'

Abby continued. 'The thing is, he's based in America and he says his clients would love quilts with a Scottish theme. Those are the only two I have, so he's asked me to draw up details of others I could make, and email them off to him for approval.'

'That's brilliant,' said Minnie.

'How many does he need?' asked Pearl.

'A lot.'

The women looked at Abby.

'But there's only so many thistles and heather one woman can sew,' said Abby. 'I was wondering if any of you would like to help. If we made one quilt each, that would fill the order. I'd tell him they were your quilts and the money would go to you. I think he'd be happy with this idea.'

Several faces lit up with interest.

'I have a thistle print quilt,' said Pearl. 'It's not on the website, but it's folded in my quilt stash. It's not purple and green though, it's shades of grey and cream, very classy. Lovely quilt weight cotton.'

Abby's response was immediate. Pearl's quilting was gorgeous. 'Take pictures and send them to me so I can show him.'

'I'll do that later tonight,' Pearl promised.

Judy stood up and ran out shouting, 'I'll be back in a tick.'

Abby was concerned.

'Don't worry,' Minnie assured her. 'Judy's fabric stash in one of her wardrobes is a goldmine of materials for every quilting quandary.'

'Is Judy okay?' Gordon asked, carrying in two large pots of tea for them.

Minnie nodded. 'Yes, we've got a quilting emergency. We're planning to take on America.'

Gordon smiled. 'It makes my offer of buttered crumpets seem tame in comparison.'

'Oh, no,' Minnie insisted. 'I think we could all do with a bit of crumpet.'

Grinning to himself, Gordon went to butter them while the ladies continued their plans.

One member had a quilt with a Scottish gorse design, and another featured a Highland stag in the one of the quilt blocks and included a tartan border.

'What about Scottish sheep?' another member asked Abby. 'Do you think he'd like a quilt featuring those?'

Ideas and suggestions circulated around the bee.

'Yes, to everything,' said Abby. 'We need to coordinate and present an interesting package to him.'

Gordon was serving up the buttered crumpets when Judy rushed in with her arms full of fabric from her stash. She dumped it down on the main table. The pre–cut bundles had some lovely Scottish theme prints.

'I couldn't carry it all, but the floral prints have thistles and heather, and the patterns for blocks and appliqué include Scottie dogs and a Scottish unicorn,' Judy gasped, slightly out of breath. 'And I'm sure I've got a Highland cow in my wardrobe somewhere.'

'I don't doubt it, Judy,' Gordon commented and then hurried away smirking.

'I'll keep that comment in mind, Gordon, when you want me to make new quilted table runners for your shop,' Judy called after him jokingly.

'A slice of your favourite cream cake coming right up, Judy,' he said.

Judy spread the bundles of fabric on the table. 'We could divide these out between us, and the patterns are handy.'

'I love unicorns,' Pearl piped up. 'I'd like to sew a quilt featuring our national animal. I'd be happy to do a unicorn with needle turn appliqué.'

Judy gave Pearl the pattern, and then divided out the others.

Abby made a note of their plans. And then she asked Judy, 'What was your news?'

Judy paused and put a pile of pre–cut squares down. She smiled at Abby. 'The boutique hotel owner phoned me. He's delighted with the quilts. Now he wants us to do a repeat order, this time with a Christmas theme.'

'Wow! That's great,' Abby cheered.

'So apart from sewing unicorns and sheep, we're going to have coordinate our Christmas quilts,' said Judy.

'Snowmen!' Pearl announced. 'I have a snowman quilt, double bed size.'

'Okay, that's one,' said Judy. 'Any others, or will we have to stitch from scratch?'

'I have two floral quilts,' said Abby. 'One has poinsettia embroidery and appliqué, and the other is a festive flower and holly print. Both single size quilts.'

'Do you have the embroidery and appliqué patterns for the poinsettia?' Minnie asked her.

'Yes, and I have several embroidery patterns for holly, Christmas robins, a gingerbread house, lots you can use,' said Abby. 'And a snowman embroidery pattern if you're interested, Pearl.'

'Yes, I'll have that, thanks,' Pearl replied.

One of the ladies spoke up. 'I'm not sure I can keep up with everyone because I tend to sew slow. I have quilts stacked at home that I've made, so I have those ready, but I may only be able to make one new quilt for the website.'

Minnie jumped in with a bolstering thought. 'Remember recently you were swithering whether to buy the fat quarter bundles of fabric from a new collection you wanted?'

The woman nodded. 'I try to economise on buying fabric.'

'Well, if you sold your quilts, you'd be able to indulge in buying the fabric you want. Think of it as a great way to fund your hobby while making a profit.'

The woman's expression changed. 'Yes, that's right, Minnie. I could buy what I wanted.' She smiled and nodded firmly. 'I think I could put a spurt on.'

'There's nothing quite like sewing with a purpose,' said Judy. 'But no one needs to feel stressed. We'll all help each other, and everyone can work at their own pace.'

'If I sell another couple of quilts I'm going to treat myself to a new sewing machine,' said Pearl.

'I'll hand the patterns in to Judy,' Abby told them. 'And remember to send me photos or details of quilts you have available so I can get the information to the interior designer and see if he's interested.'

Feeling fired up and excited, the women continued to chatter, sew and enjoy their tea, crumpets and cake.

Abby did some work on a new floral quilt she was making.

At the end of the evening, Abby stood outside the tea shop talking to Judy, Minnie and Pearl. Scottish music filtered out from the bar restaurant next door.

'Jock's holding another dance lesson for the men before the ceilidh,' Judy explained. 'Gordon said he's going to pop in. I think he's upstairs getting his kilt on. Shawn and Euan are already there.'

'My cue to skedaddle,' Minnie said, giggling. 'I don't want another peek at what's under Shawn's kilt.' She smiled and hurried away.

'Is Josh taking part in the lesson?' Pearl asked Judy.

'No, when I dashed through earlier, my husband said he didn't turn up,' Judy told her.

'He's gone back to his old ways of keeping himself to himself,' said Pearl.

Abby tried not to think about Josh and spoke about the forthcoming dance. 'It's only two nights before the ceilidh. Euan said the marquee goes up tomorrow.'

'Have you sorted out a dress yet?' Judy asked Abby.

'I had a look through my things and found a little black party dress that I'll wear with a tartan sash,' Abby explained.

'If you change your mind and want something, my wardrobe is available,' said Judy.

Abby smiled her thanks.

Waving to each other, Judy headed into the bar restaurant and Abby and Pearl went their separate ways home.

Abby walked alone along the shore. She didn't have a partner for the ceilidh. She didn't need one, but to go as a couple with someone would've been nice. Gordon hadn't asked her, and she was glad. He knew she liked him only as a friend and had promised him a dance.

When she reached her cottage garden the heady scent of the flowers was lovely. Night scented stock mingled with the lilies and the fragrance of the roses.

The night was so warm she slept with the windows open, enjoying the perfumed air and soothing sounds of the sea.

She watched Euan and several local lads erect the marquee in the morning while she whipped the buttercream filling for her cakes and swirled frosting on to a batch of cupcakes.

By the time she'd delivered her cakes and cycled back to the cottage, half of the work had been done. The marquee was hired from a nearby town, along with tables and chairs.

By lunchtime, the sun was burning a hole in the sky. The men, including Euan, had stripped their shirts and tops off to deal with the heat while they secured the rigging. The tables and chairs were carried in and everything set up ready for the ceilidh.

Abby spent most of her day and the following day, baking, quilting and preparing the information for the interior design customer. The bee members had sent her pictures and information about their quilts, and she collected it into a succinct pitch hoping to secure the order.

The weather forecast showed that the heatwave would continue for a few days, so in the late afternoon she went down to the shore for a swim. The ceilidh started at seven that night, giving her time to enjoy her swim before having to get dressed for the dancing.

The sun cast a burnished glow across the bay, and she walked down on to the sand wearing a white shirt over her turquoise swimsuit. The shore was reasonably busy, so she walked along to a quieter spot, kicked off her sandals, and left her shirt and towel on the sand.

She waded into the water, blinking against the dazzling glare where the sunlight made the surface sparkle like diamonds.

And then she dived in and started swimming along the shoreline, heading away from the area with the shops and harbour. The sea was clear and when she swam underwater, she saw the wavy impressions on the sand, pretty shells and pieces of coloured sea glass washed smooth by the ocean.

The heatwave wouldn't last, but according to Gordon the summer months were mild in this part of the coast, except for the occasional storm that tended to erupt before a warm spell.

Abby was so busy enjoying herself that she didn't notice the man swimming towards her. It was only when he called her name that she saw Josh.

'Abby, can I talk to you?'

Her breathing felt ragged, taken aback by him being there. She blinked away the sea water and looked into his handsome face. His dark hair was swept back and his beautiful grey eyes implored her to say yes.

She nodded. 'Okay.' Then she swam to the shallows and stood up to face him.

His reaction when he saw her standing there in her swimsuit was hard for him to hide. His heart raced, seeing how lovely she looked. He ached to wrap his arms around her. The feelings he had for her showed on his expression.

Her reaction to being so close to him was equally strong. For all the times she'd been swimming with Gordon, he didn't make her feel the way Josh did.

The water trickled over Josh's leanly muscled body, and she gazed up at him wondering what he wanted to say to her.

'I wanted to talk to you about what happened recently with Keera,' he began.

Abby's defences went up as she tried to protect herself from feeling a stab of resentment through her heart.

'What about her?'

'We parted on acrimonious terms, as many couples do when they split up. We were never sworn enemies though, and when she told me the trouble she was in and that financially she could be ruined, I felt obligated to help her out. It was easy for me to do, and saved her business. Unfortunately it caused a rift between us, Abby.'

'I understand your decision to help her. You shared a past. I get that. But I'm not comfortable with the idea that she can keep coming back into your life when it suits her—'

Josh cut–in. 'She's promised never to come back.'

'And you believe her?' Abby sounded incredulous.

'Keera's always been a roll of the dice. She's so adept at slanting the truth she doesn't even realise what a manipulator she is.'

'Why would you date someone like that?'

'Why does anyone become involved with the wrong person?'

Abby didn't want to start transferring that answer on to her own run of romantic disasters.

Josh straightened his broad shoulders and stood there, gazing down into her blue eyes that still bore a hint of misgivings.

'I'm finished with Keera. Our business is complete, over, done with, never going down that road ever again, lock the door and throw the key away.'

'Are you sure?' she asked him.

He went to elaborate, but then he saw a smile play on her lips and realised she was fooling with him.

He smiled. 'Yes, I'm sure.'

'Okay, but why didn't you say something sooner?' she asked.

'I thought you'd become involved with Gordon. I saw you together, swimming, having fun. You looked happy with him, and he seems to care about you.'

'I'm not romantically involved with Gordon. We're just friends.'

The relief washed over him. 'And I was going to talk to you the other day down the shore, but Euan was there. It was always bad timing.'

'Well, we're okay now.'

'So, where do we go from here?'

'I was hoping to go to the ceilidh.' She shrugged. 'But I don't have a dance partner.'

'Are kilts for the men a requirement?'

'No kilt, no ceilidh.'

'I'll get kilted up, and see you tonight. I'll pick you up at the cottage.'

Abby watched the muscles in Josh's glistening wet body ripple as he strode away up the shore. Her heart ached just looking at him.

She then swam along to where she'd left her things, and headed to the cottage.

After showering, she dried her hair smooth. The black party dress hung on the wardrobe door ready for later. Abby looked at it and reconsidered.

She made an urgent phone call.

'Judy, I have a dress emergency.'

'Pop along right now, Abby.'

Judy's wardrobe doors were wide open as Abby arrived.

'I'm assuming it's for the ceilidh tonight?' Judy was already picking a couple of suitable dresses. A pretty little tartan number and a burgundy dress with a tartan sash.

'It is.' Abby paused. 'I'm going with Josh.'

Judy looked at her, eyes wide. 'You've made up with him?'

Abby nodded and then started to smile.

Judy threw her arms around Abby and gave her a delighted hug.

'In that case, it's time to break out something special.' Judy pushed aside the other dresses and racked through to the back of the wardrobe where a dress hung encased in a protective cover. She whipped the cover off and held the dress up.

Abby loved it instantly. 'Oh, this is too gorgeous for me to wear.'

'Nonsense. This is a designer wear silky tartan dress I bought. I've never had the occasion to wear it. I sometimes bring it out and look at it.' Judy twirled it on the hanger. 'It's beautiful, isn't it? I love the way the skirt flows. Perfect for dancing.' She held it up against Abby. 'This is an ideal length for you, similar to the tea dress.'

She handed it to Abby.

Abby loved it. The fabric felt wonderful.

Judy smiled. 'I think you should try it on.'

Abby smoothed her hands down the beautiful tartan dress and tried not to feel so nervous. Her hair was pinned up at the sides with clasps, and her shoes were comfy flats.

She jumped when Josh knocked on the front door of the cottage.

'Calm down,' she muttered to herself, and then opened the door to let him in.

Josh stepped inside the cottage. He wore his kilt, white shirt open at the neck, and his sporran hung around his waist. He'd been advised by his staff to forgo his waistcoat and jacket due to the heat.

Her heart thundered with excitement seeing him standing there in her cottage looking so tall, fit and handsome.

He smiled at her. 'You look beautiful.' His sincerity shone through. The urge to kiss her was overwhelming, but he didn't. Instead, he followed her into the lounge where the patio doors were open. The night air felt hot.

He glanced around. He was familiar with the interior of the cottage, but was interested in her sewing set up and the stash of fabrics so neatly piled on the shelves.

'So this is where you sit and sew your quilts.' His interest was genuine. 'It's very well organised.'

'Speaking of organised...' she checked the time. 'The ceilidh begins at seven. We don't want to be late and miss the start.'

Abby picked up her clutch bag ready to go.

Josh glanced out at the garden. 'We could take the quick route, if you're up for it.' There was a glint in his eyes and a challenging look.

'Okay,' she said without knowing what he had in mind.

Clasping hold of her hand he hurried her outside to the back of the garden. Without warning her, he jumped over the fence and then held his hands out to her.

'Step up on the bottom strut of the fence and hold tight to your bag.'

She'd barely set foot on the fence when he reached across and lifted her over it. His strength made it seem easy, and her dress didn't even brush the top of the fence.

She gave an involuntary gasp.

Instead of putting her down, he kept her in his arms and carried her over the grassy field to the marquee.

Abby made no objections and wrapped her arms around his shoulders.

One of the older farmers attending the marquee doorway smiled and commented to Josh. 'Getting in some practice carrying your young lady over the threshold, Josh?'

Although this was their first proper date, Josh smiled at the man and then gazed at Abby. 'Yes, I do believe I am.'

147

Abby blushed and smiled at Josh as he put her down gently, and they walked together into the marquee.

A live band played, gearing up for the first dance. Couples were lining up on the dance floor, and across from them Abby saw Minnie with Shawn and waved over. Minnie waved back and looked happy to be with Shawn who kept a hold of her hand and looked proud to be with her.

Judy also waved over from near the bar. Her husband had helped to set it up. A light buffet was provided, but everyone was eager to get on with the dancing. Jock put his arm around Judy's waist and they hurried on to the dance floor.

Clasping hands, Abby and Josh began dancing, joining in with the fast pace of the other couples. The music was lively and the marquee was filled with the sounds of the band, and cheers and laughter. At one point Josh was partnered with Pearl, and they laughed as they danced together.

There were moments when Abby danced with Gordon and then with Euan before circling back to Josh.

She would always remember this night, she thought, and the happy smiles on the faces of the people she now called her friends. And Josh, handsome Josh. He made her heart melt just looking at him and she enjoyed his company.

The ceilidh was a success. Abby and Josh spent more time on the dance floor than sitting at the sides sipping a cool drink. But that's why they were there, to let their hair down, forget their misunderstandings and become lost in the joy of the dancing.

As the evening concluded with a lively reel and couples partnered up for the last dance, Minnie whispered to Abby.

'You and Josh look so happy together. You're a fine couple.'

'Thank you, Minnie,' Abby whispered, and then said, 'Has Shawn been behaving himself?'

Minnie giggled. 'No. I'm having a great night. He's been kissing me. I'd forgotten how nice that is.' She confided further. 'I found out what he had for me in his sporran.' She showed Abby the lovely thistle brooch pinned to her white blouse. 'Shawn made this for me. It turns out he's got a bit of creative streak in him, so I think we're going to get along well.'

Abby smiled warmly. 'I'm happy for you. We'll talk about everything soon.'

148

Minnie nodded, and then was swept away by an enthusiastic but caring Shawn.

'What was Minnie whispering?' Josh asked Abby.

'Girl talk. But she says we're a fine couple.'

Josh pulled her close and gazed smiled at her. 'What do you think?'

'I think so.'

He was so close, and for a moment she thought he would kiss her. Then he frowned. 'Did I hear Minnie whisper something about kissing?'

Abby nodded. 'Shawn's been kissing her, and she has no objections.'

Josh gazed longingly at Abby's lips. 'If I wanted to kiss you, what would you say?'

Abby smiled up at him. 'I'd say yes, Josh.'

Without any hesitation Josh pulled her close and kissed her longingly.

They smiled at each other, and then an announcement was made.

'Take your partners for the last dance, folks.'

Abby and Josh joined hands.

The last dance extended into another two before the ceilidh finished and everyone filtered home into the night.

The side gate to Euan's field was open, allowing people to take the route down to the shore road.

'Want to take the longer route?' Josh asked Abby.

She glanced towards the cottage that was nearby. 'I'm still up for a challenge.'

Smiling, Josh lifted her up, swirled her around, causing her to squeal with laughter, something that didn't go unnoticed by Minnie and Judy. They waved over at her and she waved back as Josh walked away with her.

He carefully placed her over the fence, then paused, waiting for Abby to say goodnight or invite him in.

'Would you like a cup of tea before you go home?' she offered.

'Yes, thanks.' Josh jumped over the fence and followed her inside.

While Abby prepared the tea, Josh looked at Abby's quilts that were folded in the lounge beside her sewing machine.

She peered through at him, noticing he didn't want to touch any of the fabric in case he ruined her work.

'It's not precious,' she said. 'You can handle the quilts and have a look through my fabric stash if you want.'

He lifted some of the fabric, studying the prints, and admired her quilt work.

Abby brought the tea through and handed a cup to him.

Josh smiled at her and drank his tea. He made no move to compromise her now that the dancing was over and they were alone in the cottage. She sensed he wouldn't take things further, not yet.

'Do you enjoy working here in the cottage?' he asked her.

'Yes, it has a good feel to it, and I love being able to work with the patio doors open and step out into the garden. And it's so close to the sea. It's ideal, and I feel happy here.'

'I'm glad.' He really was.

They chatted about her quilting and design work and she told him about the progress she'd made with her website sales and those from the quilting bee venture.

He finished his tea. 'Great work, Abby.' He headed out into the garden to leave and then paused. 'Would you like to come up for afternoon tea at my house tomorrow?'

'Yes, the same time as before?'

He nodded and smiled at her. 'Thanks for a great night.'

He walked away towards the fence to take the quick route home. The edge of Euan's field led to the pathway.

She walked out with him, and thought he was about to climb the fence when he suddenly pulled her close to him and kissed her passionately.

Releasing his hold on her he said, 'I really care about you, Abby.'

Breathless from the feelings his kiss stirred in her, she smiled, and then watched him jump the fence and disappear into the night.

Over the next short while, Abby enjoyed several afternoons at Josh's mansion, and they spent time dating and getting to know each other well.

Abby continued her baking, and had secured the interior design deal for herself and the quilting bee ladies. So the members were kept busy sewing and selling quilts, enjoying their bee nights together, chatting about gossip and of course buying new fabric. The Christmas theme quilts weren't due to be ready until later in the year, so the only quilts needing to be finished within a deadline were the Scottish theme quilts, but the ladies shared the work between them and had fun.

Abby kept her promise to Gordon to remain friends and helped him advertise his confectionery. The quilting bee nights continued to be popular at his tea shop.

Eventually, there came a time when Abby had dinner with Josh at his mansion and he invited her to stay overnight. The evening was warm, and they'd been standing outside on the balcony gazing at the view.

'I love you, Abby,' he said, wrapping his arms around her.

'I love you too.'

Josh's firm lips brushed against hers, and she felt the strength of his lean body press against her.

They spent their first night together in his bedroom, becoming a close couple, and talked about planning a future together.

The silk sheets in Josh's bed felt wonderful as Abby lay there in his arms, watching the evening sky arch over the sea.

And she fell asleep with thoughts of their new life together...

In the days that followed, Abby thought about the gift Netta had given her — a fresh start at a new life in the lovely cottage by the sea. All Netta had asked for was that her baking and cake recipes would not be forgotten. In Abby's safe keeping, they never would.

Although Josh's mansion was to become her home too, Abby continued to own the cottage where she could enjoy her quilting, and build a small business from the hobby she loved.

But more than anything, she loved Josh and he loved her.

End

About the Author:

De-ann Black is a bestselling author, scriptwriter and former newspaper journalist. She has over 80 books published. Romance, crime thrillers, espionage novels, action adventure. And children's books (non-fiction rocket science books and children's fiction). She became an Amazon All-Star author in 2014 and 2015.

She previously worked as a full-time newspaper journalist for several years. She had her own weekly columns in the press. This included being a motoring correspondent where she got to test drive cars every week for the press for three years.

Before being asked to work for the press, De-ann worked in magazine editorial writing everything from fashion features to social news. She was the marketing editor of a glossy magazine. She is also a professional artist and illustrator. Fabric design, dressmaking, sewing, knitting and fashion are part of her work.

Additionally, De-ann has always been interested in fitness, and was a fitness and bodybuilding champion, 100 metre runner and mountaineer. As a former N.A.B.B.A. Miss Scotland, she had a weekly fitness show on the radio that ran for over three years.

De-ann trained in Shukokai karate, boxing, kickboxing, Dayan Qigong and Jiu Jitsu. She is currently based in Scotland.
Her colouring books and embroidery design books are available in paperback. These include Floral Nature Embroidery Designs and Scottish Garden Embroidery Designs.

Also by De-ann Black (Romance, Action/Thrillers & Children's books). See her Amazon Author page or website for further details about her books, screenplays, illustrations, art and fabric designs.
www.De-annBlack.com

Romance books:

Cottages, Cakes & Crafts series:
1. The Flower Hunter's Cottage
2. The Sewing Bee by the Sea
3. The Beemaster's Cottage
4. The Chocolatier's Cottage
5. The Bookshop by the Seaside
6. The Dressmaker's Cottage

Sewing, Crafts & Quilting series:
1. The Sewing Bee
2. The Sewing Shop

Quilting Bee & Tea Shop series:
1. The Quilting Bee
2. The Tea Shop by the Sea
3. Embroidery Cottage

Heather Park: Regency Romance

Snow Bells Haven series:
1. Snow Bells Christmas
2. Snow Bells Wedding

Summer Sewing Bee
Christmas Cake Chateau

Sewing, Knitting & Baking series:
1. The Tea Shop
2. The Sewing Bee & Afternoon Tea
3. The Christmas Knitting Bee
4. Champagne Chic Lemonade Money
5. The Vintage Sewing & Knitting Bee

Action/Thriller books:
Love Him Forever
Someone Worse
Electric Shadows
The Strife Of Riley
Shadows Of Murder
Cast a Dark Shadow

Colouring books:
Flower Nature
Summer Garden
Spring Garden
Autumn Garden
Sea Dream
Festive Christmas
Christmas Garden
Christmas Theme
Flower Bee
Wild Garden
Faerie Garden Spring
Flower Hunter
Stargazer Space
Bee Garden
Scottish Garden Seasons

Embroidery Design books:
Floral Garden Embroidery Patterns
Floral Spring Embroidery Patterns
Christmas & Winter Embroidery Patterns
Floral Nature Embroidery Designs
Scottish Garden Embroidery Designs

Printed in Great Britain
by Amazon

14375962R00092